THE PRIDE LIST

EDITED BY SANDIP ROY AND BISHAN SAMADDAR

The Pride List presents works of queer literature to the world.
An eclectic collection of books of queer stories, poems,
plays, biographies, histories, thoughts, ideas, experiences
and explorations, the Pride List does not focus on any specific
region, nor on any specific genre, but celebrates the great diversity
of LGBTQ+ lives across countries, languages, centuries and
identities, with the conviction that queer pride comes from its
unabashed expression.

Omar Youssef Souleimane

The Last Syrian

TRANSLATED FROM THE FRENCH BY
GHADA MOURAD

LONDON NEW YORK CALCUTTA

**PAP
TAGORE**

The work is published with the support of the
Publication Assistance Programmes of the Institut français

Seagull Books, 2024

First published in French as *Le dernier Syrien*
by Omar Youssef Souleimane

© Editions Flammarion, Paris, 2020

First published in English translation by Seagull Books, 2024

English translation © Ghada Mourad, 2024

ISBN   978 1 8030 9 344 4

British Library Cataloguing-in-Publication Data
A catalogue record for this book is available from the British Library

Typeset at Seagull Books, Calcutta, India
Printed and bound in the USA by Integrated Books International

The Last Syrian

1

This is an old story.

Some merchants had found a child in a well, near the pyramids of Egypt. They decided to take him to the slave market where he was sold to the high steward of the pharaoh who, having no descendants and fascinated by the intelligence of this little boy, adopted him.

The boy grew up in palaces and became extremely handsome. His bewitching face aroused an illicit passion in his adoptive mother.

One day, she gathered her female friends and gave each a knife while the young man brought them fruit. Unsettled by the sight of this magnificent being's beauty, the women slashed their hands. 'This is not a human being, this is an angel!' they exclaimed. Overwhelmed by desire for the young man, the mistress of the house wanted to lock him up and reserve his charms for herself. He defended himself, so when the adoptive father arrived, the woman accused the young man of attempting to rape her. Although the lie was

3

eventually uncovered, the high steward threw the young man in prison anyway.

Youssef had heard this story dozens of times. 'That's why I named you Youssef, my sweetheart. So that you become beautiful, like the prophet Joseph,' his mother would say to him on winter nights, as his head rested on her knee while she ran her fingers through his hair. 'He worked miracles, could foretell the future from people's dreams, and was finally released from prison, because he was honest, patient, and never abandoned his principles.' These were the last words the child heard every night before he fell asleep.

*

This is an old story.

In March 2011, when Youssef took part in the first demonstrations in Damascus, he had the impression that the cry for freedom raised against the al-Assad regime after forty years of silence and fear was a miracle more powerful than that of the prophet Joseph. No god had provoked it; it was the pure product of outrage. Bouazizi set himself on fire in Tunisia to say no to the dictator Ben Ali and, in response to his sacrifice, a massive wave of protests swept through Egypt, Libya, Yemen and then Syria. No one had foreseen this tsunami of anger.

After one of the demonstrations ended, a police officer chased after Youssef, who ran into a building, dumped his bag, and took off his jacket. Upon leaving the building, he pretended to be a beggar and even asked the policeman for a coin on his way. Even today, he does not understand how he dared to do this or how his pursuer did not recognize him. Since then, he feels like everything around him is nothing but a movie. This thought comes to him even in the toughest of times and makes him laugh.

He has not returned to Damascus since that episode. He misses the capital that inspired him so much. Despite the risk of being arrested by the intelligence services, it would be an exciting adventure to go back there and meet new comrades. For him, Damascus is like a mirror, a sun between two clouds; there he feels eternal. Every time he visits, he feels like he has found a part of his soul. He loves to walk around the old town for hours; this is the only place where he doesn't obsess with the future—a bird in flight that he pursues relentlessly.

Youssef is dressed in his best clothes. If he were to disappear from this world, he would like to be elegant. Elegance is his means of resistance.

2

Joy sweeps over Youssef as he watches the scenery pass by through the bus window. At this moment, nothing can disturb his happiness or shake his strength. All will be well—this idea inflames his heart. From his seat, he watches his reflection in the glass and meditates on his first name: 'I have no connection with this prophet, I don't even know if this is a true story and I don't care. He guessed the future through dreams, but the rebels make them come true, and that is what matters most.'

The space between his seat and the one in front is tight. This is nothing new; he often has this problem with his long legs. When he was little, his classmates nicknamed him 'The Spider' and kicked him.

He thinks of his friends from the group Qalb, whom he met in Homs a few months ago. People like him are activists fighting for a different future, eager to bring together all the different groups of Syrian youth against the regime. These students, who are often brilliant and active, scientists as well as literary types, come from several universities. They were all fed up with the corruption there; children of high-ranking military officers could, for example, have access to exam questions beforehand. These activists converged from the start of the revolution and, after much discussion, decided to establish a political movement. For Youssef, the primary objective is to avoid a civil war. 'We must resist the regime peacefully, reject all forms of violence and remain independent. We are not a political party that wants to seize power.'

The bus passes a golden statue of the former president Hafez al-Assad, smiling, his arm raised in a salute. 'Soon this land will be free,' Youssef says to himself. 'You'll see, we'll kick you in the ass, we'll crush you and throw you in the trash.' He reads the news headlines flashing on his cell-phone screen: 'Protests in the south, despite the army siege of the regime. Nineteen-year-old boy killed on the coast by sniper bullet.' He switches to international news: 'Islamist militias fight the government in the Libyan capital. Democratic elections for the first time in Tunisia. A new sex scandal around Berlusconi.'

He turns his head to the left. A man in his fifties is eating sunflower seeds while watching a third-rate film being screened inside the bus. Youssef never liked this custom of showing bad movies in crowded vehicles; you couldn't hear the actors' voices. Also, these typical 1970s movies always had a happy ending: the hero married the heroine while the bad guys ended up dead or imprisoned.

3

At the beginning of October in Damascus, the heat mixes with the cool, fresh air; it feels like you are living in two seasons at once. The sky is clear; the city is bathed in a soft light.

Next to the Al-Hamidiyah souk, one can see the statue of Saladin on horseback, brandishing his sword as two soldiers stand by his side, dragging prisoners captured on Crusade. Behind the statue stands the citadel. Its battlements are pierced by the rays of sunlight, which recall old civilizations, wars, victories and defeats. For centuries, these places have told the story of this city, once occupied by the Romans, Mongols, Turks . . . all of them gone. The city has endured; it is still beaming.

Tired of waiting in front of the souk, Mohammad walks away, pretending to start a telephone conversation. Hiding behind junk items hung in front of a shop, he scrutinizes passers-by. Every time one of them turns towards him, he jumps.

He regrets having arranged this rendezvous so close to his clothing shop; he risks running into one of his clients. He's been working there for years. It's a family business run by his father and grandfather before him, who spent their lives there. A good reputation is essential to keeping customers. What would they all say? Would they call him a faggot? Who would dare to enter his shop after that?

He notices a street vendor. He is afraid. These people often work for the intelligence services. He has known them for a long time, ever since the time they arrived at his home under the cover of darkness. He couldn't even make out their faces. He vividly remembers their military shoes in the hallway crushing his father's face: 'You want to start a coup, asshole?' As they took him to their car, Mohammad clung to his mother's dress, shaking. He could feel urine running down his legs. He did not understand anything. He had only one feeling: horror. This is still the case whenever he crosses paths with an intelligence man. Mohammad's mother had run after them: 'Where are you taking him? Stop! Wait!' His father had yelled at her: 'It won't be long. I'm sure it's a mistake. Don't worry!'

Ever since that night, every time Mohammad asked her where his dad was, she would tell him he was travelling. The years passed; they continued to live in their big house. His mother was hard on him. She kept telling him, 'You're not like the others. You're the child of a hero. You must follow his example.' He would nod, then ask her permission to watch *Cinderella*, his favourite cartoon. Once, when he had joined other children on the pavement to play football, his mother came and beat him in front of his friends before leading him back inside. For her, the street was a wild world where he was not allowed to venture out on his own.

It's not yet time for his rendezvous, but as usual, he's early.

4

Although this was not a common thing to do, she chose to rename herself Josephine. Not only out of love for Josephine Baker but also for the name's meaning: one who brings people together. No one knows her real first name. When asked, she laughs and says, 'I have forgotten.'

During her first year in college, she made friends everywhere: in Aleppo, Homs, Damascus, on the coast. Now she travels constantly from one place to another to see them. Every time she meets someone, she feels like she is rediscovering herself. Her happiness resides in solving their problems; today she is trying to find a solution for those of her country.

She has lived in Damascus for three years, having left her parents' house on the coast to study English. A simple excuse to flee her family. She was the only girl growing up in the presence of three brothers, suffocating in a small village where everyone knew one another. For her, Damascus was a new world where she could breathe. Her father had initially refused to let her go, but she managed to persuade him. 'I'm going to be a teacher, and you can brag about me to your friends.' He went on to provide everything she needed for her studies.

Josephine feels stressed for no particular reason, but it's always like that. She walks into a shop, chooses beauty products—very quickly, without even looking at them—pays, and dashes back out to the street. She is not far from Chaalane, her neighbourhood. She runs with a bag on her back, her cell phone in hand, which she looks at all the time to reply to the dozens of messages she receives. A young man calls out to her: 'What are you doing tonight? I want to lick your pussy.' She raises her middle finger in his direction without even looking at him.

A text arrives from Khalil: 'I'm on your street. I'm waiting for you.' She smiles. She likes the simple message, knowing he can go without her. She runs her tongue over her lips, deciding what to answer. He has the key, like all her friends. 'My apartment belongs to all of you. As for me, your arms are my only home,' she tells them every day. She met Khalil soon after setting up Daou, a group of activists in the capital. It was in April, a month after the start of the revolution. 'We must bring together all the young activists from all regions and focus all energies like a laser to destroy the al-Assad mafia.' This was an idea inspired by her childhood: once in their garden, she and her friends had used a magnifying glass to set leaves on fire. Khalil had been one of the first to join her group. He loves working with her.

He is ready to go days without sleep to organize a demonstration if this girl, Josephine, is there. She replies, 'Go upstairs, I'm coming.'

5

The elevator is very small. Youssef steps aside to let Josephine pass. She refuses, but he insists. She pushes him by the shoulder: 'Go on, honey, forget the cliché, I'd rather be by the door.' She slips her hand into her bra. 'Don't look, it's not a striptease!' she says, bursting into laughter. She stares into his eyes but finds no desire. She keeps her hand under her shirt, without moving, as she forgets what she is looking for. She didn't imagine Youssef's reaction would be so cold, so calm. He looks at her in turn, completely indifferent. She takes out a pen and hands it to him.

'What do I do with it?'

'What do we do with a pen, we dance?'

'Why are you giving it to me?'

'A gift. Not to write, to film.'

She takes off the cap, pulls out a tiny digital camera, puts it back in place, presses the button of the pen and fixes it on her breast pocket, saying, 'I love you, Youssef, you look beautiful!' He notices some graffiti spray-painted at the bottom of the elevator: a red heart pierced with an arrow. He shows it to Josephine and replies: 'I know, here's the proof.'

6

Headphones hanging over his shoulders, the elegant Khalil rubs his eyes every now and then, glancing at Youssef as he exchanges jokes with Josephine. These two seem close; they even walked into the apartment together, laughing. Dozens of questions swirl in Khalil's head; all he knows about Youssef is that he lives in Homs. Since the events, he has tried to unravel the true character of people to be sure that they aren't spies. But he can't gauge this new visitor. Rachid, another activist lying on the couch, smokes hash and tells Khalil, 'When we see you, we think you have a date with a princess, not that you're going to a political meeting.' This isn't the first time Rachid has made this kind of remark to him. When they first met, Rachid touched his arm and said, 'What a good-looking guy!' Khalil smiled, but today he's not in a good mood. An overwhelming melancholy is suffocating him; he doesn't understand why, which makes him even more sad.

The bright balcony lighting reflects off a glass table in the heart of the living room. The sofas are arranged chaotically. Josephine's coat lies next to her shawl. The open closet is overflowing with clothes of all colours. A painting on the wall shows an old man walking, his face turned towards the living room as if he were observing Josephine. She takes a USB stick from her pen and plugs it into her computer on the table. Khalil, Youssef, Rachid and Josephine clearly see and hear the 'I love you, Youssef' whispered a little earlier. Josephine turns towards the young men and scrutinizes their reactions to this new technology. Rachid exclaims, 'Wow!' Youssef's eyes are on his cell phone: 'It's already three o'clock, and I have an appointment in an hour. Can we talk about the matter at hand?'

Khalil tries to grab a glass of water from the table but knocks it over. The sound of the glass shattering on the floor makes him jump as if he heard a thunderclap. It was really quick; he feels like the glass fell by itself. He gets up to fetch a mop but Josephine stops him: 'Forget it, it's OK.' She tucks a lock of rebellious hair behind her ear. 'We are here to organize a big demonstration in Homs bringing Sunnis and Alawites together. In the capital, the regime has already imprisoned a large number of activists. This hasn't happened yet in the town of this young man standing here before you.' She points to Youssef. 'The situation is very different there. There aren't any intelligence services in the old town any more. The residents have managed to drive them out.'

Rachid pounds his fist on the table: 'Bravo! You can't even imagine how much I dream of living there! We can walk around, we can say whatever we want out loud, without the fear of being arrested by the police—that is paradise! That is real revolution, that is . . .'

Youssef cuts him off: 'Not quite. In retaliation, the regime has set up checkpoints and numerous snipers in Alawite neighbourhoods that target Sunni civilians. Hatred is everywhere; it is only growing. Some have even taken up arms.'

'Very well,' Khalil replies, 'we need weapons to protect the demonstrations. We are peaceful, yes, but we need a deterrent force to scare these butchers! These criminals have everything: cannons, warplanes—but they're cowards. The other day a little boy shouted near a checkpoint, "The rebels have arrived!" The soldiers fled like rabbits.'

Pensively, Youssef caresses the red petals of the flowers on the table. 'If everyone takes a Kalashnikov, we'll head straight into a civil war!' Khalil says, 'The solution is for the soldiers to desert and create a new army to support the revolution.' His lips tighten; his eyes betray his nervousness and tension. 'Smoke up, my darling, everything will be fine,' Rachid suggests to him. But his comrade in arms doesn't respond; he has a strange feeling towards Youssef, who is sitting in front of him like a statue, full of confidence. He knows what he wants, but he's so sombre. Maybe this newcomer isn't the problem, maybe it's just that he's not feeling well today. Without a word, Khalil walks out onto the balcony, skirting the broken glass on the floor. Nothing is clear in his mind. He regularly sees in his sleep images of cities swallowed up by a sea of sand. At that moment, he imagines it is happening, precise and sharp as truth.

7

On 15 March 2011, Mohammad was in his shop which they called 'Liberty'. Unthinkingly, he shut all the windows, turned off the light and hid in the dressing room for an hour. In the days that followed, he wondered: Where was Syria headed? Was the regime going to fall? And would the revolution be stifled? No one had the answers to these questions. So, like many, he's waiting to see what the future holds. But today he is full of desire, hesitation and anguish as he awaits a young man. He is in the new part of town, not far from the courthouse, where protesters are taken and driven for several hours before being put in prison. This building scares him, but Mohammad likes the two palm trees at the entrance; they are very tall, even taller than the courthouse. Suddenly, three prisoners come out of the building. They are dressed in convicts' clothing, white and black stripes, feet and hands in heavy chains. The intelligence agents beat them with sticks. Mohammad turns his head away. Violence is everywhere around him. He's exhausted and doesn't want to wait any more; it's already ten minutes past his rendezvous time, anyway. Police may be monitoring the Habibati website where he contacted this young man. He thinks about that word, *habibati*, 'my beloved woman', the most famous gay dating site, and wonders who gave it this name.

Youssef appears, walking towards Mohammad, and gestures for him to follow. Mohammad is worried; he is shaking. His fear gradually dissipates as he approaches Youssef. He tells himself, 'This is a man! A man. Not a woman. Who would suspect that we're here for a happy hour of fun? People can imagine we are friends, nothing more.' The streets are crowded with pedestrians, bystanders. The clothes seller is torn between fear and excitement. He doesn't know this man. What if he's an informant? Who knows?

On the terrace of Café Nawfara, behind the Umayyad Mosque, there is another world, that of the old town. Calm reigns everywhere, as in prayer. In some of the alleys, the leaves of the trees form shaded arches, and flowers seem to emerge from the old walls. Those who do not walk in silence and do not have an eye for beauty would never notice these sights.

Youssef smiles, his face lifted to the sky, as if it was there that he saw Mohammad's face. The joyful atmosphere makes them want to make love. The two men set out for the refuge that they will be for each other.

8

Mohammad's house is in the heart of the working-class Jaramana district in the south-eastern outskirts of the old city. 'The people here come from all parts of Syria. Everyone knows everything about everyone: your profession, where you come from, the name of each member of your family, etc. They are very good in the art of intelligence.' At the main entrance to the building, Mohammad feels more secure. As far as the neighbours are concerned, Youssef and he are simply friends.

'This is my one-bedroom palace. I've been living here for a year,' he says, sitting next to his guest. The two young men talk about everything except what got them here. Youssef looks at him with confidence and serenity, and that troubles Mohammad. He feels uncertain and fearful. He hasn't had sex with a man for a long time. His last encounter had been very brief. He had contacted a guy online, and they had arranged to meet at the Byblos cinema. At the ticket counter, they bought two seats in a small box, on a bench without armrests. Mohammad was not interested in the film, but a nude scene still disturbed him: he imagined that the heroine was stroking him while he himself kissed the hero's back. He moved closer to his neighbour and touched his thigh, then gently brushed his penis with his fingers. Then the stranger took his in his hand. They were at the back of the hall. It all happened very quickly. They never saw each other again. And since this encounter, Mohammad has not been with anyone.

With Youssef, it's different. He is overcome with desire but doesn't know how to proceed. Youssef can see that Mohammad is panting, yet he dares not go any further. He takes his time. They breathe in unison. Mohammad rambles on about everything and nothing: 'Here, you can find a room that isn't too expensive. For the same space, you have to pay three times that price in the city centre.' Youssef listens, his chin resting on the palm of his hand:

'And there's enough space for us to meet in peace?'

'I'm happy living in a small studio.'

'Me too, but it has to be very bright.'

'Yes. You can also find very bright apartments here.'

'How about you? What do you like?'

A long silence sets in. Mohammad's heart is pounding; it shows in the bulging veins of his neck. But nothing alters in his sweet face and his eyes, full of childhood and sadness, that close as he murmurs, 'Kiss me.' Youssef starts with his lips, the lower one, then the upper one. He undresses Mohammad, takes off his own clothes. He pulls him onto the bed, buries his head in his chest. He would like to disappear the better to be reborn. He wants to cover with kisses every little part of this body offered to him. He lies on his back and says, 'I want you.' Mohammad takes out a tiny bottle of oil. Slowly, he enters Youssef, then lies down on top of him. Two waves of desire unite on the mattress.

Mohammad's perfume awakens an old memory in Youssef, of the time when he still lived with his two sisters and his mother. In the morning, he would go out into the garden with his slate and draw a brick house, a river and a wheat field. He liked to think that when he grew up, this drawing would come true. His mother would then come out to hang up the laundry; the smell of cleanliness would mingle with that of eucalyptus. Youssef could only see her bare legs behind the laundry. She would vigorously shake each item of clothing before hanging it up and drops of water would fall on his drawing. 'It's raining on my house!' he would shout. His mother would laugh and bring him back inside to have breakfast. At that time, his universe had no limits.

'Youssssef . . .' Mohammad pronounces his name in a weird way—the s sounds like a bird's twittering. Relaxed, he sits down next to him; tears of joy run down his cheeks. His cell phone rings, and a song of praise for Bashar al-Assad rings out. Youssef's face tightens. Mohammad hands him a glass of fruit juice, gets up, and opens the window without pulling aside the curtain. 'What is most important to the Shiites?'

Youssef hesitates, then asks, 'What do you mean?'

'Secrecy! The Shiites hide their beliefs in a hostile environment. I am like them. Most customers who come to my shop support the regime.'

Stroking Youssef's chest hair, he continues: 'My father was arrested in the 1980s. He was reported to the intelligence services and accused of being a member of the Muslim Brotherhood even when he had nothing to do with them. We never knew who reported him. He spent ten years in jail and emerged a broken man. My mother died shortly after he came back to us. He is a very tired man now; I will do anything to spare him any more pain. I even got engaged to make him happy. Her name is Sarah. She's charming—with intense eyes and a very slim waist, which I like. Her hands keep moving when she talks, and I think that's cute. Sexually, I feel less and less attracted to her. But when I see my father's smile, I silence my deep desire for men. He thinks I'm going to get married and give him grandchildren.'

Youssef laughs, shrugging. 'Sounds like he's the one who's getting married and not you. Does he know you sleep with men?'

'Are you kidding? He would renounce me if he came to know. All he knows is that I rented this apartment for my upcoming marriage.'

'And in the meantime, we make love on this bed intended for your marital antics!'

'Yes. To be honest, you are not the first. Several people have been here. Women and men . . . What I'd really like would be to have a man and a woman in my bed together.'

Youssef starts getting dressed. This lost young man makes him anxious yet moves too. 'I would love to be part of your threesome, but I don't touch women.'

9

At the bus station, Youssef takes Mohammad's hand in his, but Mohammad shakes free:

'Are you crazy?! Do you want to go to jail? I don't!'

'The police are too busy cracking down on demonstrations. They don't have time for us.'

Most of the buses are small, old and in poor condition. Not only are these smaller buses much cheaper than the large ones, but you also don't need to make a reservation. Men shout, 'Homs! Aleppo! Daraa! Come on, we're leaving right now!' chasing travellers and asking them where they are going. Anytime someone brings a new passenger to a bus, the driver gives them a small amount of money. Mohammad hates this bustle; he wants to run away. The station is big, but not big enough for the crowds that throng the place. While Youssef buys his ticket, Mohammad carefully scans his body, thin and elegant. His blue-and-white shirt goes well with his red pants. He feels like he has known him for a long time, or at least that he has met him somewhere before.

The two men walk towards the waiting line; Mohammad has a lot to say, but he finds it difficult to speak. 'I'm afraid of what the future holds. What we're doing is not right, we will go to hell. I'm not that religious, but I still believe in God.' He says this as if someone else is speaking for him.

Without looking at him or turning around, Youssef replies, 'We are not hurting anyone!'

'I know. But the Prophet said, "If you see two men together, kill them!"'

'Maybe he was jealous of us. Anyway, religion is rubbish. Homosexuality has been around forever, you know. Several caliphs were gay.'

'Yes, Yazid Ibn Mouawiya and Al-Walid Ibn Abd al-Malik. Some intellectuals too and even poets: Abu Nuwas, Ibn al-Rumi and Abu Firas al-Hamadani. But that's not where my problem lies. I don't know if I'm gay or not.'

'Nothing is set in stone, everything is moving. No one knows what will become of you. We change every minute, every second. And if one day you stop having sex with men, if you choose to stay away from all the taboos, that will be something respectable.'

Youssef sets his luggage down in front of him and continues, 'Be like the cloud, no one can decide for it where and when it will rain. Remember when we were teenagers and the grown-ups warned us about masturbating? They told us that if we did, we would contact serious diseases—tuberculosis or skin cancer—and that we'd end up being impotent. Growing up, we found out that was nonsense! Our parents were brought up with the forbidden; they are ridiculous. They haven't really lived their lives. But they have to let us live ours.'

These words restored Mohammad's confidence and dispelled his worries, just as a storm drives the foam out of the sea. He doesn't like goodbyes and doesn't want to linger. Without a word, an agreement is formed between them: *No matter what happens, we will continue this story, nourish this bond.*

10

Mohammad sits in front of his computer and immediately opens the VPN program that lets him go incognito and elude the intelligence services. He remembers his first conversation with Youssef on the Habibati dating site.

Mohammad entered his nickname, 'The Sweetie', and his age, twenty-five. About ten Internet users were online: the Addict, the Sexy, the Chief, the Maso, etc. Only Youssef used a genuine first name. Mohammad sent him a private message and waited a long time for a response that did not come. As he was about to get up to make coffee, a beep stopped him: 'What are you looking for?'

'To meet somebody. And you?'

'To get to know each other. And maybe go further. Where are you?'

'In Damascus.'

'I'll be there in a few days.'

'Let me see your photo first.'

In the photo Youssef sent him, he was fair-skinned, with a small beard and very expressive brown eyes. Mohammad, in turn, posted a snapshot taken by Sarah when they first met at Damascus University, introduced by mutual friends. She had taken a series of selfies with their friends and finally asked Mohammad to sit on a bench looking towards the sun. She captured the moment without noticing that behind him, on a wall, calligraphy proclaimed: 'You are our president forever, Bashar. We love you.'

Mohammad lies down in the dark and tries to sleep without thinking about what happened that day. Tomorrow he will see Sarah. He puts his pillow over his face. When his father was in jail, he did this when he wanted to cry, so his mother wouldn't hear him. He still does it, no longer to hide his sobs but to protect himself from a world he finds unjust.

11

Every evening, the government cuts the power in Homs' Old Town. It started when people began protesting in the streets, so the locals wouldn't go out. But the power cut had the opposite effect: having nothing else to do at home, the residents began gathering outside more and more. Meanwhile, those living close to pro-regime neighbourhoods discreetly pulled electrical cables to help themselves to free electricity.

Youssef and Bilal, another activist from Qalb, are preparing a small dinner of omelette, cheese and olives. They are at the Centre; this is how this ground floor has been baptized. This name circulates in the al-Khaldiya neighbourhood, especially when someone is injured. The Centre is made up of two apartments. The first serves as a makeshift hospital with a single bed and an X-ray machine. It's a substitute for the government hospital, which is located on the other side of town. Youssef spends a lot of time in this apartment to film the victims. The second apartment has two rooms, making it possible to organize meetings there, or prepare reports, or simply rest.

Youssef and Bilal eat seated on the floor. The room is lit by candlelight. Photos of their comrades, those killed or arrested, are pasted on the walls, where the word FREEDOM can also be read, drawn in blue-and-red calligraphy.

Bilal does not speak. This young man is small and very lively. One day, while watching the protests in Tunisia on TV with his family, he became fascinated by a new slogan: the Arab Spring. He then closed the bicycle repair shop he was running and followed the call of the revolution, or the rebels, or the democracy, or . . . whatever. All Bilal knew was that the protests were at the heart of his existence. Since then, he has spent his time thinking about how the regime should end. His relatives had warned him not to participate in the movement: 'This will not lead to anything. You will die. Besides, you have no political experience.' But Bilal had not listened.

He questions Youssef to see if it is certain that their comrades from Damascus will come. The latter replies that nothing is certain given the situation. He opens Google Earth and shows Bilal the streets through which the protesters plan to enter al-Khaldiya. The two heads come closer, almost glued. Bilal, excited, stares at the map when suddenly the screen shakes, and the sound of a very loud explosion rocks the neighbourhood.

12

Mohammad enters the Chez Nous restaurant in the city centre and goes to the table at the back to be as far away as possible from the customers at the bar, who are talking loudly and clinking glasses. His date with Sarah has left him stressed; it's been like this for a few months. They no longer see each other without arguing. This time, he's decided to be brave and forthright: he's going to tell her that he can't go on with her any more.

When Sarah arrives and sits across from him, a heavy silence follows. She slowly swirls a spoon in her cup. She adjusts her veil, putting it back in place, and opens her mouth to speak but hesitates.

'I have good news. More and more of my law-school friends are taking part in the revolution.' Mohammad doesn't really listen to her. The moments spent with Youssef return to him. He can still feel his lips on his chest, his fingers around his waist and even the smell of his skin. He is afraid Sarah would notice it, that she would have an intuition that there was another man.

'What are you thinking about?'

'Us.'

'I called you yesterday. You didn't answer.'

'I was at the shop.'

'At 10 p.m.?'

'Sometimes I stay late to do the books.'

She knows he's lying. Neither wants to continue the discussion. For Sarah, the most important thing is to preserve their relationship: everyone around her knows they are together. For Mohammad, she is proof that he is still a normal person. 'Are you going to stay grey for a long time?' Regardless of what she means by 'grey' today—neither for nor against the regime—this colour is his favourite.

'I've told you a thousand times that your protests have nothing to do with me. You're free to do whatever you want.'

'Free? If my family knew what I'm doing, they would kill me. My dad would, for sure. He's already threatened me several times: "If you join in this bullshit, I'll slit your throat from ear to ear like a sheep's."'

13

Reading and sex are what save Mohammad and keep him from falling into depression. At his parents' house, there was a large library full of books on religion and history, two topics that interested him. At the age of seven, he was already climbing the shelves, grabbing *The Thousand and One Nights*, taking his father's glasses, and doing as he had seen him do: read with a very serious air. He didn't understand anything, but he felt good. His mother would get angry when she caught him at it. His father's library and glasses were sacred. No one, without exception, was allowed to touch her absent husband's much-loved things.

At school, the other children avoided Mohammad. For them, he was the traitor's son. The little boy escaped solitude thanks to books, his only friends.

While in college, Mohammad had a passion for stories about homosexuality in the Abbasid era, in the eighth century. He loved the way their very poetic language described the bodies of these men and their seduction games. As he read, he imagined walking the farms around Damascus, meeting a young man, and making love to him in nature. He felt like he was living with these simple, happy, rich people, who sometimes had more freedom in their days than he did today.

One story had particularly appealed to Mohammad: that of the Abbasid Caliph al-Wathiq in the ninth century and his lover Muhaj. Like many, the latter worked in the palace but, unlike the others, he was the prince's favourite. Thus, whoever wished to send a petition to the master of the house had to go through him. Every night, Muhaj covered his lover's body with perfume, embraced and kissed him before letting himself be penetrated. He left the caliph free to satisfy his every desire. Muhaj knew how to excite the caliph and drive him mad with happiness. Once his master had calmed down, Muhaj placed a hand on the caliph's chest and all his requests were granted. One morning, however, they had an argument, though no one knew why. The consequences were immediate: Wathiq, in despair, no longer cared for his empire. Muhaj resented the caliph. But the ministers managed to reason with him and the life of all Muslims in the kingdom returned to normal after this passing quarrel.

Mohammad rereads this text, which he knows by heart. It's the end of the day. He feels empty, and he would like to live a story like this. While closing the shop, he decides to go to Sebki, his favourite garden.

14

From: Youssef <youssefcadi@gmail.com>

Sent: October 7, 2011

To: Mohammad <mohammadamir@gmail.com>

Subject: Following up on our first meeting

I no longer know if I came to know you through Damascus or if you made me discover it. I have a lot of friends in this city, but I have never loved it so much as in your arms.

On the evening of my return to Homs, someone threw a bomb in the al-Adawiya neighbourhood, where pro- and anti-regime people live side by side. Fortunately, no one was hurt, and only one shop was set on fire. Either way, people are used to the sound of explosions. At night, government supporters open fire on the blocks of buildings where their opponents live. Opposite, the others respond, and the exchange of fire continues until dawn. With sunrise, people calm down, come out of their homes and invite each other for tea on the pavement. Together, they insult both the government and the Opposition. Complicity takes hold behind this rhythm: friends by day, enemies by night.

That's not what worries me, but rather the faces that recently appeared in the Old Town, those of violent people who shave their moustaches and keep their beards. Some come directly from the jails of the regime that freed them to tell the world that the revolution is Islamist. They are paid by Turkey and Saudi Arabia to wave black flags with white writing on them: 'There is no god but God.'

The Opposition in exile is doing nothing. When the Syrian National Council was created, I inquired about its members. I found out that most of them are members of the Muslim Brotherhood, who have sought no change since the revival of political Islam in the 1920s. All they're interested in is coming to power. It would then be an opportunity for them to establish an Islamic state. Democratic-sounding slogans are broadcast to help them achieve their ends, but we are not so dumb as to believe them.

In the midst of all this sadness, you appear to me like a meteor in a dark galaxy. I know you think of me too. This morning, I saw a flowering tree in front of my house. I had never noticed it before.

15

Not far from Bab Sharqi, Khalil contemplates the tidy clusters of tomatoes in a shop stall. They come from the south of his city, Daraa. At the beginning of the revolution, the regime soldiers mocked the people who were rebelling in this province: 'All you know of life is the cultivation of tomatoes, and you ask for freedom!'

In his childhood, Khalil would accompany his parents to the farm, where they would stay all day picking tomatoes with the people of the village. Overwhelmed by the heat, the child's cheeks would turn red. His parents would tell him to go and rest in the shade, but Khalil would refuse, only to show them that he was no longer a little boy, that he had become even stronger than them.

Since then, when he is away from his family, every time he sees a tomato, a bitter taste fills his mouth.

Bab Sharqi is his favourite neighbourhood in Damascus. Christians and Muslims have always lived side by side and shared the beauty of this place adorned with wrought-iron lanterns. Before sunset, the traffic calms down, the air seems cleaner and passers-by look more serene.

He was due to meet Josephine this afternoon, but she cancelled their date with a 'I'm very busy,' which immensely upset Khalil. Today he wouldn't have the chance to share the warm world of this woman, who makes him feel safe. The young man wanders for two hours until his feet hurt. Then he receives another message: 'Rachid is quitting his studies, you must see him. Make him change his mind, he listens to you more than to anyone else.' He phones Rachid to arrange to meet him at 7 p.m. But it's already 7.30 when Khalil sits on a bench and tries to keep busy with his cell phone. He takes a look at Facebook and then switches to Twitter. His friend still doesn't answer.

When Rachid finally arrives, he is carrying two bottles of beer. He looks like a cat that stole his master's meal. 'I swear to you, on my mother and my sister, it's the traffic that made me late!'

A generous human being with eyes filled with eternal love: that is what Rachid becomes when he drinks. He hands his friend a bottle, but Khalil refuses it and gets up. He begins to walk, looking at his feet. Rachid hops alongside from one black stone to another, avoiding the white ones.

'Rachid, they told me you left college, is that right?'

'Yes. The police at the entrance scare me. They search everyone. Plus, an intelligence-services office has just moved into the premises. Students are arrested every day.'

'That's not a reason! You have a wonderful future awaiting you: you'll be a doctor. Don't waste it!'

The alcoholic, as his friends call him, leans his shoulder against a small wooden door.

'I hate the word "prison". I only have to hear it to think the end of the world is near, you understand? I am not a hero or a brave man, the only reason I participate in the revolution is for the happiness I find there. When I am in a protest, I feel like there is still beauty on this planet, and when I shout "Freedom!" I get drunk! I swear! As if I had drunk ten shots of whiskey!'

The young man says 'Freedom' in a loud voice. As they hear a noise from the shop next door, Khalil grabs his friend's arm: 'Stop, you're going to cause a scene.' But Rachid continues in the same tone: 'We must be happy, my friend. It's a good way to stay alive and piss off this bitch called death. I don't understand why you are always so sad. When I see you, it seems like you carry all the world's troubles on your shoulders. You don't drink, you don't smoke and I think you don't fuck either.'

'Shut up!'

'Thanks, I love you too. But I assure you that I understand what's happening to you. You're in love.'

'Alcohol makes you a philosopher . . .'

Rachid has already drunk both bottles as they approach a church. 'It's true I drink a lot, but I feel things and I understand the people I love. Yes, I understand you all: you,

41

Josephine and Youssef. I even understand the stones!' He picks up a stone and kisses it. 'It's very old and tired. It's melancholy. I think it's longing for a bird that has migrated far away.'

He walks towards the pavement; he stumbles and falls.

Khalil holds out his hand to help him up, but Rachid gets up on his own. 'I hurt the Earth. We have to tread gently on her. She is our mother, and we are her lost children.'

16

At the checkpoint, they do not search Josephine. Not only because her identity card indicates that she was born in an Alawite coastal town known for its support for the regime, but also because of the ring on her nose, her bright smile, her stylish hair and her black beanie that make her look very pretty. Even when Josephine isn't smiling, she is beaming; no one could imagine her organizing protests behind the authorities' backs. She is aware of it and she plays it up. She is even convinced that anyone who exudes such positive energy succeeds and gets through danger unharmed.

The soldier glances at the car and asks Josephine where she is from and where she is going. 'I'm a student, I go to Homs University,' she always replies. The soldier then complains about the difficulties of his job: 'I've been here for three months and I haven't had a single weekend off, no rest. I feel all this exhaustion, just so these dogs can stage a demonstration. We're all sick of it. Even the pay has dropped a lot, the government is out of money.' As he speaks, his

Kalashnikov slips off his shoulder. Josephine wants to shout at him and tell him to revolt and turn his weapon against the real oppressors; instead, she just looks at the gun.

'You look exhausted,' she whispers to Youssef as she enters the Centre.

'I'm working a lot right now, but that's not why I'm exhausted. Last week a fourteen-year-old was killed. The state sent a group of mercenaries to the Alawite neighbourhood. Massacring civilians amuses them.'

'What can we do?'

'I'll start by making myself a coffee. Do you want one?'

'Yes, thanks.'

Josephine lights a cigarette.

'In my suitcase you'll find food and all the medicine you need.'

She takes off her coat.

'You need to rest, Youssef. The human body is like a machine—the more energy you give it, the more it will serve you.'

For Youssef, the only way to rest would be to go to Damascus, to Mohammad.

His scent still envelops him.

Coffee overflows from the coffeemaker.

'What's wrong? I can see your mind is somewhere else.'

Running one hand through her hair and resting the other on her waist, she approaches his ear and whispers,

'You're thinking of a woman, aren't you? Tell me, I won't be jealous, I promise.'

'A woman . . .' only reminds him of his mother, his sisters, and of Josephine, who is his best friend and with whom he feels free to talk.

'I am like Rimbaud.'

'I know.'

He looks at her, not understanding how she found out.

'You're the only one out of all the guys I know who's never hit on me.'

'And how does this make you feel?'

'I love Rimbaud. He's a great poet, I love his radicalism. Plus, he's really handsome.'

'You know what I'm talking about.'

'Look, I had sex with girls when I was in high school and, I swear, most of the women I know have, too.'

'For me, it was just an experiment, but others followed suit. Today I prefer men, that's how it is. I don't think we get to decide.'

'Yes, but society . . .'

'You just told me that you're like Rimbaud. In his day, it was the same for him. Look around you, our people live permanently in hiding. Everyone has desires that they keep to themselves, and we are told that there's only one legitimate way of life: get married and have children, otherwise you're a pervert. Our society is sick! Look at the number of girls who have been circumcised—is that not a crime? How will they experience their sexuality? No one dares to talk about it and everyone is lashing out against homosexuality. It makes no sense!'

'We have a long way to go. When we talk about homosexuality, people shout in response: "Allah Akbar!" We're rising up for democracy while others are calling for the caliphate to be restored.'

'That's their problem, not ours.'

'What are we then?'

'Forsaken. Islamists hate us because we are secular; the regime, because we are rebels; and the politicians, because we are sincere. They call us traitors, infidels, heretics because they don't yet know what it means to be free.'

17

In the Sebki Garden, Mohammad sits and observes his surroundings. He looks at three young men not far from him: one of them is wearing very tight trousers and a red tee, a chain hangs from his pocket to his knees; the second has a short beard; the third is tall and muscular. They are listening to rock on one of their cell phones. He would like to approach them but does not have the courage.

A smiley face followed by a red heart reach him on his Bluetooth messenger. He replies with 'I want to fuck tonight and I have a house.' He then waits, but his cell phone remains quiet.

Mohammad is convinced he will meet someone here. Two guys are behind him on a bench. It's 10 p.m. and the others are gone. Here, in the heart of the city, people no longer fill the streets with their conversation. Little by little, the cold settles in Damascus and makes Mohammad want to kill himself.

Being inside someone right now would pull him out of his sadness. He longs to make love—this violent desire has taken hold of him; it never leaves him any more.

He imagines himself with a man, in the dark: he bites his neck, grips his butt with all his might and claws his back with his fingernails; the other screams with pleasure. Mohammad doesn't give a damn that the neighbours hear them. He climaxes and sees nothing of this world, only his cum on his partner in the dark.

His blood is boiling. Nature around him feeds his desire for sex. He would like to sleep with a man behind these trees. A policeman walks slowly through the garden. Suddenly, Mohammad is sure the policeman is there to arrest him— maybe he has even been followed for months? Are they aware of his sexual adventures with men? But doubt prevents him from fleeing. The policeman may not be there for him; if he starts running, the man may become suspicious. The policeman finally walks away. Mohammad asks the two young men on the bench behind for a light. He likes one of them; even if he is not really handsome, he will do: dark-haired, he wears a bracelet of seven colours around his left arm. As the fellow's friend goes to buy a Coke, Mohammad wants to take a chance and tell him what he has in mind, but the other takes the initiative.

'I live on the university campus, where I study English. I'm passive, and you?'

'Active.'

'Do you have a room?'

Mohammad looks around; he can't believe it. His hands are shaking; his breath quickens.

'Yes, in Jaramana.'

'Let's go?'

'And your friend?'

'Forget him, he left so we'd be alone.'

18

Adel is the person who lives closest to Youssef in the al-Khaldiya neighbourhood. Before the revolution, the two were not friends at all. The young man was born here; he never finished his studies. Being a taxi driver, he gets to know all the local residents, who appreciate him for his loyalty.

Though neighbours, Adel and Youssef had never spoken to each other. Every morning, while cleaning his cab in front of his house, Adel would watch the sleek, showy student pass by. For his part, Youssef had the impression that Adel was a rude and violent man; he had heard him use vulgar words several times while drinking tea with his friends.

At the start of the revolution, before there were many protesters, Youssef was filming a demonstration and recognized Adel's face in the camera view. It was his neighbour, the taxi driver. He hesitated to say hello, but Adel came right up and shook his hand:

'Well done, what you're doing is wonderful.'

'But you are . . .'

'Yes, I'm with the revolution. Does that surprise you? Do you think that because I didn't go to college, I should stay at home?'

'No, no, on the contrary.'

Over the course of the gatherings, the two men who were sizing each other up until yesterday became friends. Adel would share his networks with Youssef and Youssef would teach Adel his public-speaking skills and power of persuasion.

When his brother was killed by a sniper during a demonstration, Adel was in shock for days, repeating the now-famous phrase in his neighbourhood: 'Between us and Assad, there is nothing but blood.' Youssef was there for him; he promised him revenge, but fair revenge. He explained that after the end of the regime, they would organize a trial to judge those responsible for this blood-bath. This gruesome ordeal brought to light Adel's will-power, which proved stronger than the bullets. The day after his brother's funeral, he woke up and resumed his daily existence as if nothing had happened.

When Adel's wife knocks on the door, he gets up and goes to get the tray she has prepared for them. Youssef doesn't like this precaution; he didn't come here to ogle Adel's wife. But he understands. He knows him well, this man, who spent his youth in the company of prostitutes and alcohol, and for whom everything changed when he got married. Adel became a believer.

When the taxi driver hears from Youssef that there will be Alawites at the next protest, he hesitates.

'What if they are regime spies? How can we trust them?'

Youssef knows the people of the Old Town well; they are ready to change their minds as soon as someone talks to them about humanity. 'I can vouch for that, trust me, we need them to bring down the regime. We can't do anything alone, we have to be united, strong.' Adel nods. He accepts it without another word but categorically refuses to allow the protesters to raise money for the families of the victims.

Due to his upbringing, Adel does not accept help from anyone. He is used to giving, not begging. He also doesn't want people in his neighbourhood to receive money from just anyone. It could hurt their dignity, especially after losing their children. But Youssef knows how to convince him: 'These donations come from the merchants of Damascus. It is their way of showing that they support us, since they cannot participate in the revolution.'

As always, Adel gives in to this sincere and determined man, whom he considers his little brother: 'All right, I'll talk to them, and bring you a list of their names.'

19

From: Mohammad <mohammadamir@gmail.com>

Sent: October 10, 2011

To: Youssef <youssefcadi@gmail.com>

Subject: Following up on our first meeting

Islamists are present not only in Homs, but here too, in the suburbs of Damascus. I know where they come from and how their ideology was forged, because they lived among us and they grew up in our schools. Especially at the Al-Fatah Institute, where Islamist sciences are taught. Their project is simple: to establish a state that applies Sharia law.

Sarah has changed; she has grown distant from me. I think about her a lot, but she refuses to see me. I wanted to make love to her, to melt the wall of ice between us. After we met at the university, I suggested we spend the night together.

But she always refused, telling me each time, 'That's not how I was brought up.' She must— and wants to—remain a virgin until marriage.

I met a guy at Sebki Garden and he came to my house. No sooner had the door closed than we were naked. I pushed him onto the bed, but he got up, took my cock in his mouth and started sucking it. A true professional! I couldn't stop thinking about you.

I couldn't wait any longer, I grabbed him by the shoulders and pulled him up. He lay on his stomach so that I could be on top of him. He closed his eyes as if he couldn't feel a thing. As soon as I came, he smiled, got dressed and left silently. I spent the rest of the night lost between you, Sarah and my desire.

When can we meet again? Give up this thing you call revolution! I'm scared for you. Sarah also goes to the gatherings. The last time, she wanted to go to Douma. In this town, the soldiers are shooting at the demonstrators, but she does not care. She's gone completely mad.

One of my neighbours was arrested two days ago. There's a guy living on the ground floor who spends all his days in front of the building and monitors everyone's comings and goings. He is an informer for the regime. He was the one who reported him.

20

On weekends, at eleven in the morning, the Chez Nous restaurant is almost empty; that's when Mohammad prefers to go there. He orders a coffee and rereads the story of Caliph al-Amin. In his youth, the caliph lived in Baghdad where many *ghilmans*—ephebes—were in his service. They used to dress in tight-fitting colourful outfits. Little by little, the caliph got rid of all his maids. Shocked by his attitude, his mother, Zubaida, hatched an ingenious plan: she brought very beautiful young women, cut their hair, dressed them like young men and ordered them to walk around the palace.

Al-Amin was won over and he dismissed his ephebes. He was proud to present these women to his visitors. Zubaida wanted to preserve the status of women in the palace and her stratagem became a veritable tradition in the homes of princes. The young women were called *ghulamiyyat*s. Is this why some men in the Middle East like to dress as women?

No. Youssef told him that as a child he loved to cross-dress. When the rest of his family was away from home, he would take clothes out of his mother's and sisters' closets and dress up and put on make-up in front of the living-room mirror. He would look at himself and enjoy talking like a girl. That is when he felt fully himself. Once, when he was playing with his three sisters, they dressed him up in a red skirt. He was happy; they laughed and photographed him on the bed from several angles as if he were a model. Their mother suddenly entered the room. The harshness of her reaction only fuelled his desire to continue this behaviour.

Mohammad finishes his coffee and, as usual, puts his cup next to the saucer. He's never been passive with a man; that is not where he finds his pleasure. But ever since he met Youssef, he's been thinking about it. He glances across the street as a woman with sunglasses walks by. He never liked people who wear sunglasses. He doesn't know which way they're looking or what they're thinking or feeling. Seeing someone in sunglasses makes him feel he's in the presence of a ghost.

21

About twenty people sing at the Centre, their voices echoing in the neighbouring streets. Sahida's voice stands out, very clear, strong and moving. The singer of the revolution, as young people call her, is seventy years old. In the early summer of 2011, she started writing revolutionary lyrics and setting them to music. She lost two of her sons in a demonstration in April in Homs. The demonstrators were leaving the Old Town for the first time and heading towards the city centre, when the intelligence services had opened fire, shooting one of her sons in the stomach. His brother held him back and tried to carry him to the pavement, but he too was shot in the neck and collapsed before reaching it.

When Sahida learnt that her two sons had died in each other's arms, she said, 'They were always inseparable, they never left each other.' Since then, she no longer found any meaning in her existence. To give back meaning to her life, she joined the anti-regime organizations. She usually covers her head with a white shawl; her face still retains some memory of her beauty.

Khalil stands next to Josephine. Their arms touch; she doesn't move. He is moved, overwhelmed with joy by this tiny contact. 'Now is the time,' Adel tells them as he enters the room. Everyone stands up but they don't stop singing: the members of Daou, Qalb and the Alawites of Homs. With his ear to his phone, Adel leads the way to check the route and make sure the streets of al-Khaldiya are safe.

The Alawites participating in the revolution wear masks so as not to be identified in the videos by their families or pro-Assad neighbours. Camera in hand, Bilal sits on a Suzuki motorcycle that serves as a platform. Rachid holds a bottle of beer in one hand and a banner in the other: 'Down with Bashar al-Assad!' 'You'll go down before he does! Hide that! Nobody drinks here in public!' Youssef yells at him.

Josephine's sign proclaims: 'The bullets have killed only our fear!' She hands it to Khalil for him to brandish as well. Josephine climbs up next to Bilal to proclaim on the microphone: 'We have the right to live freely like all other peoples on this earth. Our children have the right to grow up in safety and to choose their president and their representatives.'

People cheer and applaud her. Women throw rice and flowers from the balconies. This tradition, usually reserved for weddings, amazes Josephine. 'We want to try the killers and free the prisoners.'

Many passers-by join the procession, surprised at this movement led by a woman and devoid of any Islamist flag.

Sahida begins to sing, 'Bashar, son of evil, leave quickly—this country does not belong to you.'

The demonstration is a pilgrimage for freedom; the crowd heads for the court, repeating sentence by sentence after Sahida: 'Free, free, freedom, we will have our freedom, in spite of you, Bashar!' Their voices carry, some raise their hands to the sky, others put their palms on the shoulders of their neighbours and dance in a circle. The trees in the garden at the centre of the square move in the wind, giving Youssef the impression that they are dancing with them. A light drizzle falls. A young man with a drum climbs up next to Sahida and plays along with her singing. People applaud, forgetting the time and the danger that watching them in the street entails. They are like children who have just been given a gift.

All around, the demonstrators in charge of security look worriedly in every direction and check every street leading to the square to be sure there is no police movement. It is not easy to end the parade, but it is essential to ensure a minimum of safety for the participants. Youssef grabs the microphone and repeats, 'Go home. We will resume tomorrow!' They return to the Centre, tired yet elated. The locals follow this strange, happy group with their eyes, while evening descends upon the neighbourhood.

22

They prepare the meal together. Josephine gets to work: she dices the tomatoes into small identical pieces before putting them in the pan; Youssef crushes the garlic and Khalil mixes the tomatoes with the red meat.

The kitchen is small, but the songs have not left their lips and make them feel like they are organizing a big party.

From the meeting room, Bilal calls them to come and watch the video of the protest. Youssef joins him while Khalil stays with Josephine as she adds spices to the dish. He takes advantage of being alone with her to ask her to spend the evening with him on the terrace:

'The night is clear, and you like the full moon.'

'What about the snipers?' she said, lowering the gas flame. 'I would rather be in a quiet place.' She stirs the rice with a spoon, trying to hide her smile. 'There aren't many of us. The night will be calm.'

23

The sky is clear and the stars are visible although it is the middle of autumn. A breath of air gently lifts the curtain, the smell of the season's first rain permeates al-Khaldiya. Cypress and eucalyptus trees stand still despite the sound of bullets, making you forget that a war is raging.

Rachid places a sheet of paper on a cushion, mixes weed and tobacco on it and rolls it into a large joint. He takes a long drag and keeps the smoke in his lungs; almost nothing comes out of his mouth. Through the window, he notices a lighted balcony opposite, which he does not take his eyes off.

The others are chatting excitedly, and their words are nothing but joy and fervour. 'Remember the slogan: "The cosmos is Assad's lair"?' said Josephine.* They all laugh.

---

* In Arabic, *assad* means lion. In 1987, military pilot Mohamed Fares spent a few days aboard the Soviet space station Mir. Upon his return, he became famous in Syria and the propaganda services wrote this sentence in luminous letters on the slope of Qasioun, the mountain overlooking Damascus, to demonstrate that President Bashar al-Assad was behind this feat and that the extent of his power reaches even the sky.

She then told them what had happened a few days earlier in Damascus: 'About ten young men and women gathered in the city centre and chanted slogans against the regime. They filmed themselves. There were also Alawites among them. It didn't take more than a quarter of an hour before the police attacked them with knives and dogs. It was nevertheless a blow to the intelligence services, and I am sure Bashar is shaking in his palace. I hope that tomorrow there will be more Alawites marching against this asshole!'

Youssef continues, 'I wonder how to make sure that the Alawites stop being afraid for their future and demonstrate alongside us. In Ottoman times, in the nineteenth century, they were not allowed to be civil servants and lived isolated in their mountains. They are considered infidels by most Sunnis. In fact, when an Alawite passed through a Sunni town, he had to do so with his head bowed, otherwise the traders would beat him up. Don't forget that Hafez al-Assad gave them control of the army when he carried out his coup. This bastard, who is himself an Alawite, told them that he was there to protect them. And today it is his family who threatens them that if they don't support him and if the regime loses power, the Alawites will become slaves again.'

Josephine leans towards him, her golden hair brushing against his shoulder. 'Yes, I know, my dad was in the military all his life. He cannot be persuaded to revolt against the regime. My mother too. They are afraid of the Sunnis. They think that as soon as the regime falls, the Sunnis will crush them like flies.

'We must think how to take this fear out of their heads. If the National Council doesn't do its job, it is up to us to do it, everywhere and all the time. It must be said that the revolution serves democracy for all Syrians, regardless of their religion or ethnicity.'

'What you say is sublime, friend. You represent me, not the National Council.' She pauses for a few moments, puts her hand on Youssef's knee: 'I'll write a call on this topic and send it to you to post on social media.'

'You want to revolt on the Internet?' Rachid asks, offering her the joint.

'The regime has set up a "digital army". These bastards receive big salaries for insulting us on social media and presenting us to the rest of the population as terrorists, using all kinds of language. We have to organize to face them and explain to the world that the revolution we are leading has nothing to do with the Islamists. The movement will not be limited to the Internet! We will create real opposition within Syria.'

'Dream on!'

The last words make Khalil, who had remained silent until then, react: 'Who told you that we are not dreamers? Only a year ago, no one would have imagined that such a mobilization was possible in Syria. We have been controlled for fifty years by a dictator.'

'Spin, spin and hit me before the police arrive,' Rachid hums. He stretches his legs. 'When is the regime going to end? I'd like to resume a normal life—spend time by the sea, between the orange fields and the beach, bathe during the day, and drink in the evening while watching lighthouse beacons reflected on the waves . . .'

No one comments. They all share these hopes. Rachid continues, 'I ask myself: why do we have to be victims who are arrested, injured, killed? Why do we have to make this sacrifice to have a real country? Why isn't the situation simpler? Doesn't love alone open a path to freedom without the need for violence?' He looks at Khalil wryly.

The silhouette of a woman passes quickly behind the curtain before disappearing. Rachid follows her, eyes half-closed. 'Damn the Sunnis, the Shiites, the Alawites, and all the other religions and ethnicities! Damn the regime and the Opposition!'

With his eyes open, he imagines himself lying on the sand, rays of sunlight breaking through the leaves of a palm tree and caressing his face. A few steps away, girls are walking, their feet in the water. 'I want to see women in bikinis again, for me that is worth more than all the flags.'

24

Adel can't get to sleep. He keeps thinking about his brother who was killed, about his wife lying next to him and about their little one, just two and a half years old, or thirty months old, as he likes to say when someone asks him. He doesn't celebrate his son's birthday every year, but every month. The child holds a ball in his arms, his head propped up under his mother's armpit. This is the only way he agrees to fall asleep. They breathe at the same pace.

He thinks of Youssef; he wants to protect this young man. After everything they've been through together, Youssef has become a mirror reflecting his own face, that of years ago, when youth looked like a thunderstorm and his life was less hard. At one in the morning, the streets of al-Khaldiya are deserted except for a few men patrolling the area to protect the neighbourhood from incursions by intelligence services and thieves.

Adel leaves his house, flashes his torch three times and waits for the three young men with sticks standing in the square to do the same. Everything is fine. He continues towards the Centre. He was the last person the activists expected at this hour.

The smell of hash reaches him from outside the building. It annoys him, but he doesn't say anything. They are still young, and he too did the same at their age. 'Have fun but be careful that no one sees you! Do you need anything?'

'I would like to talk to you alone,' Youssef tells him, leading him towards the kitchen. 'Have you prepared the list of the families of the victims?'

'No, they refused to accept money from people who let them down. They think these people are accomplices of the criminals—they have not even reacted or organized a single strike against the massacres. Excuse them, the blood of their loved ones is still fresh.'

'But it was not the traders of Damascus who killed them!'

'When death is everywhere, injustice prevails. It becomes difficult to talk sense.'

Adel resumes his walk; only the darkness keeps him company.

25

'Caliph al-Amin had an ephebe named Kawthar in the palace. The two men were very close. Kawthar was the favourite of the caliph, who even wrote poems to him: "Kawthar is my religion, my world, my disease and my doctor." They were inseparable and it didn't surprise anyone at the palace. Al-Amin's father, Haroun al-Rashid, had many lovers of both sexes who served him wine, sang, played the lute and went to bed with him. Al-Amin, who came to power at the beginning of the ninth century, spent his time indulging in pleasures without realizing that his brother al-Maamoun was preparing a coup d'état. He had assembled an army and was preparing to attack Baghdad.

'Kawthar was wounded in the face when he came out to see what was going on. The caliph stopped everything he was doing to attend to his lover. He wiped off the latter's blood, saying: "They've hit the apple of my eye! O God, avenge me!"'

Mohammad interrupts his reading to check his email. On the BBC website, among the news, there's a photo of

Kate. He remembers her wedding to Prince William; her white dress was tight at the waist, very classic, and the faces of the bride and groom were empty, devoid of feelings, like that of Barbie dolls. Two emotions clash within Mohammad: he is happy not to be married, but he is aware that he is not in the norm. He thinks of Sarah, who recently ran away from her family home to live with a friend. Her father had finally learnt of his daughter's anti-regime activities. Mohammad offered to come and live with Sarah, but she refused on the grounds that she was not yet his rightful wife. Deep down, he is happy with this answer, for he can no longer imagine a future with her.

A customer enters the shop and walks to the fitting room after choosing a skirt. She calls for him to come and help her zip up the garment. As Mohammad complies, she asks him what he thinks about it. He tells her that she is charming, which makes her laugh:

'I'm talking about the skirt, not me!'

'It suits you very well, especially with this white sweater.'

She turns to him with a big smile, which makes him uneasy. He apologizes and goes back to the cash register.

Maybe she wants him, and he should seduce her. But he could be wrong, how can he be sure? Besides, they're in his shop, not in a brothel. When she draws the curtain, he tells her that she is as resplendent as the sun.

He imagines her naked while she chooses a pantyhose. When she pays and leaves, a strong sense of guilt seizes him.

Why all the hesitation? Why didn't he ask for her phone number? Such a waste!

Today, for lunch, he's just going to grab a sandwich and go for a walk. He enters the al-Hamidiyah souk; in the crowd he feels as though he is lost, which allows him, in a way, to find himself. Everything is for sale here: perfumes, kitchen utensils, carpets, pottery, sabres, chiselled daggers, boxes inlaid with mother-of-pearl, spices . . . This place, which has been swarming without interruption since its creation in the eighteenth century, seems sadder lately. Buyers are no longer jostling each other, and tourists have become scarce. Yet there are a lot of people.

He then arrives in front of the Umayyad Mosque. Doves searching for leftover dry bread thrown by passers-by scatter in his presence. He doesn't stop at this familiar scene. Nearby, a child sells DVDs for 10 pounds. Mohammad walks up to him and looks at the action movies and comedies on display. With a wink, the child offers him special films. They're 100 bucks.

He continues to the citadel where the streets are less crowded. Mohammad gives the loose change in his pocket to an old beggarwoman sitting on the ground. He notices that the level of the Barada River is high, although the water is no less polluted.

To his right, a sign reads 'Hammam of King al-Zaher'. He knows that in his grandfather's days, people thronged here every Thursday before the day off. They brought a snack and spent the afternoon and evening eating, chatting and washing. But since people have bathrooms, the number of customers has greatly decreased. Despite everything, here the hammams never close. They are still very popular with European tourists. Mohammad heard that homosexuals frequent them too, but he hasn't had the courage to verify it yet. Youssef's words came back to him: 'Be like the cloud, no one can decide for it where and when it will rain.' This time he goes in.

26

From: Youssef youssefcadi@gmail.com

Sent: October 21, 2011

To: Mohammad <mohammadamir@gmail.com>

Subject: Following up on our first meeting

Today a group of activists returned to Damascus after participating in a protest here. I cried, not because I will miss them, but because it seems to me that our country does not deserve them. These young people are strong. Throughout their childhoods, they learnt that they could only live because of the fascist ruling over us. At school, each day, they chanted: 'Our president for eternity, the faithful Hafez al-Assad!' As teenagers, they memorized his speeches. As adults, they are now trying to dismantle the propaganda they grew up with.

Even bananas were fed up with the 'faithful one'. Hafez al-Assad had banned the import of this imperialist fruit which he said did not serve the fight against Zionism. Ever since I was little, I've wondered about al-Assad's issue with bananas. Did he simply dislike them, or was he allergic to them? Why did he forbid all Syrians from eating them?

Yesterday I was among the demonstrators, without really being with them. I was thinking about you the whole time; glad no one except me knew it. The electricity was cut. We lit candles even though the stars were very bright. Of course, I didn't really see them; it was only the light that reached us since they have been extinguished for millennia. These stars, born with the Big Bang, from shocks between atoms, make me think of your sex inside me. We too are exploding into a universe of desire.

I no longer go on dating sites. It doesn't interest me any more. Getting to know you was enough for me.

Beware of your neighbour, the informer! We are lucky here: there are no intelligence services in the neighbourhood. But this situation will not last. If the regime does not manage to enter the city, it will bomb it. And who can stop that?

Rumour has it that Iranian forces have entered the country. A colleague of mine filmed a tank bearing the flag of the Islamic Republic near Homs. A nice irony, coming from this regime that accuses us of being outside agents.

27

The hammam is divided into two parts—one side for women and children, the other for men. They each have three areas: the outside for eating, a sort of anteroom for resting, and the inside of the hammam for having your body massaged vigorously in the midst of intense heat.

At the entrance to the establishment, a group of men are seated on a stone bench covered with rugs. One of them, the owner, is leaning on an elbow and giving orders to employees while taking care of the cash register. From time to time he checks if everything is going well.

In the locker room, Mohammad wraps himself in two towels and then exits the small room next to the door. He walks with his head held high to appear sure of himself in front of these men. A young man in black pyjamas takes the bag containing his clothes and leads him inside.

'I'll come back with the soap. Do you want someone to rub your back?'

'No . . . Actually, yes!'

The masseur who shows up isn't like Mohammad had imagined him. He is forty years old and has a tough face. The man asks him to keep only the towel around his waist on and to sit facing the wall. He starts at the neck, pulls the horsehair glove up to his waist, pours very hot water all over his body. Noise fills the space: the dome of the ceiling is a few metres above their heads.

Mohammad closes his eyes, imagines being on the edge of a forest, in a free country. He is reading a book, his neck resting on Youssef's thigh, whose beard seems to rise from the sky. People walk around without disturbing them or paying them any attention.

The masseur reaches the lower part of his back; his hands violently knead Mohammad's muscles. When it is all over, Mohammad feels like his worries have left every cell in his body.

A voice reaches him from his left. Despite the steam all around, he makes out a European man: tall, blue-eyed, sitting just like him on the floor. The guy in the black pyjamas massages him; his fingers sneak under the towel and gently touch his sex. The light through a small window illuminates the black and blond of their hair. The European begins to gasp.

*

74

When the guy leaves, the blond man wipes his arms and turns to Mohammad:

'Marhaba! Hello!'

'Where do you come from?'

'Germany.'

Together they step outside the hammam. The German speaks Arabic with a strong accent. 'I worked at the Goethe-Institut cultural centre. My contract is finished but I am in love with this city. I've been coming here for years now, everyone knows me.'

The young man appears with two glasses of tea and a hookah. He leans over to Mohammad and whispers: 'A Westerner who smokes in a hammam, what do you think?'

'It's like a Syrian eating bacon with Queen Elizabeth II.'

Mohammad looks for a way to direct the discussion to the scene he had just witnessed between the tourist and the young man. 'Do you travel thousands of kilometres to find pleasure in Damascus? Don't you have hammams at home?'

'Yes, but in Syria it is much better than in Germany, where I don't find people who are as gentle with older men. Here, on the other hand, I feel much freer: we eat together, we drink and we make love. Besides, I love Arabs! Especially the ones with dark skin. Maybe as a European I see it differently.'

'What do you mean?'

'To you, Europe stands for civilization, peace, wealth; and the Middle East, poverty, sadness, violence. I find your country exciting. It's a hot country, you're deeply interested in bodies. The body is linked to other riches, like culture, philosophy, architecture. It might have been one of the reasons the Europeans occupied you.'

His gaze grows sad. He plays with a red ring attached to his little finger: 'But this is probably the last time I visit Syria. I no longer feel safe here.' Mohammad doesn't understand why European tourists love his country. Here, where one is not allowed to breathe without the dictator's permission? If freedom were slaughtered, would beauty still exist?

He stands up abruptly, the towel falls, he wraps it back around his waist, making sure no one has seen anything. He waves to the European who is busy putting charcoal back on his hookah.

28

As usual, before leaving for work, Adel contemplates his son. The child tries to kick a ball but only manages to fall on it. This ball is the little boy's most precious possession. Adel asks him if he needs anything. Although his son is too little to answer, Adel takes great pleasure in asking him the question.

Sukayna, his wife, is very busy today as her in-laws are coming to their house for lunch, and she is determined to clean the garden before they arrive.

Through a window between the houses, he catches a glimpse of their neighbour; even though no man can see her, she has put on her veil. The two women talk politics; they say a solution is being put in place. Every time Obama says that Assad's days are numbered, everyone repeats his words. Sukayna prefers to change the subject; she already hears her husband and the TV say the same thing all day long. She then asks her neighbour for pomegranate molasses so she can surprise Adel by making a lahmeh-bessiniyeh, the dish with minced meat and cracked wheat that is his favourite.

As she sweeps the floor, one of her earrings falls off and lands on ants clustered around a crumb of bread. The little piece of metal quickly disperses the insects. She picks it up, puts it back in place, thinking that the area of her body between her ears and her shoulders is the one that her husband appreciates the most. When they make love, this is where his lips stick together as if he were quenching his thirst after a month of drought. This single thought gets her carried away.

The little one pulls her out of her reverie by throwing his ball on the ground. She orders him to come inside the house so as not to get his clothes dirty, but it's too late.

29

Driving through Homs at noon is difficult, but Adel has to go to Hadara Street. Many are waiting for a taxi there. During the day, all kinds of people walk around the city: students, employees, traders . . . until sunset when everyone disappears into their neighbourhoods. Today at the checkpoint, the soldiers are not content just to watch and flirt with the girls as usual: they are on edge because of the clashes the night before with armed groups in the Old Town where one of the soldiers was injured.

Adel stops at the traffic light. Before him a large crossroads where a statue of Hafez al-Assad had stood before the events. The police recently decided to remove it. They feared the demonstrators who destroyed many statues in other regions would also demolish this one.

An old man selling fruit pushes his cart between the cars and the soldiers: 'Clementines, sweeter than honey! Clementines!' The soldiers order him to leave, but the old man tells them that he has been coming here every day since he started working and he continues to push his load: 'Oranges! Full of vitamins!'

The military commander slaps him and kicks the cart, overturning it and its contents. Adel gets out of his car, takes the vendor by the hand and tries to lead him to his cab, but the man pulls away: 'That's all I have to live on!' He begins to pick up the fallen fruit.

'Yes, take it all and stick it in your mother's pussy!' the soldier shouts at him contemptuously.

'Aren't you ashamed of what you're doing?' Adel interjects.

The military chief approaches him and grabs him violently by the moustache: 'What if I ripped this? You'd be handsome enough for me to fuck you!' Adel spits on him and hits him in the face. The soldier steps back, draws his pistol and fires without blinking. Adel falls, slowly, his blood, very clear, trickling in the sun.

30

From: Mohammad <mohammadamir@gmail.com>

Sent: October 27, 2011

To: Youssef <youssefcadi@gmail.com>

Subject: Following up on our first meeting

I have just remembered a story my grandmother told me when I was little. It was about how lovers dated in her day. 'The girls left their homes every Friday morning with a bucket full of laundry and soap on their heads. They would arrive at the river, settle on the riverbank and start washing their clothes. Women's hands in those days were more powerful even than those of men nowadays.' Anyway, that's what she assured me. 'The boys who worked on the farms in Ghouta, east of Damascus, would pass nearby. The paths between the olive trees and the vines were so narrow and the trees so thickly lined that they had to waddle to move forward. The girls would glance up at them discreetly.'

My grandfather, who is in love with her, rolls an apple into the river, causing a slight ripple. My grandmother pretends nothing happened. He then starts all over again and, at that moment, she looks at him. Her classmates laugh, and she feels the heat rising within and taking hold of her body. She no longer has enough focus and energy to continue her work. The mischievous boy hands out apples to all the young women and remains standing next to the one he loves. The other girls slip away to leave them alone.

Towards the end of her life, my grandmother had Alzheimer's. She had forgotten even the names of her own children. Only this story was intact in her memory and she told it in great detail.

I think of Grandma every time I log on to a dating site and use phrases devoid of warmth and emotion to contact girls or boys my age. As soon as one of them leaves, others replace her or him; it's a real computer rut. The web page would have to turn into a lake where seducers would throw apples.

A few days ago, I brought a guy to my house. His way of walking was effeminate and gave him away. Everyone in Jaramana stared at us as if they wanted to kill us. Someone even said, 'Congratulations! When is the wedding?' I didn't want to leave this man but I was afraid to continue towards home. It was a mistake: you shouldn't come here during the day. We went to the restaurant and, five minutes later, a waiter ordered us to leave or else he would call the police. Since then, I hear obscene words thrown at me every time I walk in my neighbourhood. I'm now seen as a pervert.

Sarah is in Douma. She made a deal with a rebel to bring her there. She left alone, with no money, didn't tell anyone and took only a few clothes. She was able to pass the checkpoints thanks to a fake ID card. When she arrived, she phoned and assured me she wanted to be a peaceful activist and said she had decided to work in a law firm. 'I will create the list of victims injured, arrested or murdered by the regime. I won't be far, twenty minutes by car.' Her phone call was very brief and I haven't heard from her since. After that, I saw that the regime had surrounded Douma and shelled it several times.

I'm going crazy! I don't understand anything any more. After Sarah left, I realized how much she meant to me: her words, our discussions, even our arguments—it all enlightened me. I need to have someone by my side, even if I don't agree with that person. Her absence weighs on me, I miss her. Sarah is so full of tenderness and humanity.

Her father called, begging me to do something. I told him we were on the verge of breaking up anyway. He wouldn't hear it: 'You are officially engaged! You are not the only one to decide!' He then informed my father about our discussion, which made my father's condition worse. He no longer leaves the house and now spends his days watching TV and sleeping. I imagine Sarah in Douma every day. There are Islamists among the rebels. Will she survive all this violence? I wonder if she's still alive. Disappeared? Injured? Sarah believes our generation is a bridge that future generations will cross in order to achieve democracy. I know you share this idea, but just watch what happens: the most beautiful youths in Syria are dead, and with no result.

31

The Centre is calm, with neither visitors nor wounded this afternoon. Youssef takes a nap and smiles in his dream. He is lying on his back, one arm covering his eyes. Next to him, Bilal, one hand on the keyboard, a piece of bread in the other, follows the news of the war, avoiding political articles that never seem to change: meetings of the Opposition in Turkey, a call from the Minister of Foreign Affairs about the plot against Syria, etc. For three days, Youssef has not changed his clothes—he is no longer interested in doing so—nor has he contacted his family. He even sleeps by the computer after listening for hours to speeches by Muslim Brotherhood imams about the importance of taking up arms against the powers that be in order to protect their religion. He receives a text: 'Clash on Hadara Street, someone opened fire!' He posts on Twitter while awaiting more details.

Bilal shakes Youssef: 'Get up, lazy bones!'

'How long have you been here?'

'About an hour.'

'I forwarded to you the appeal against the Syrian National Council. Josephine sent it to me yesterday.'

'I know, I've read it and made some changes. Listen: "In the name of God, we, the Syrian Arab people, declare that the National Council does not represent us and mocks us with its hollow slogans. In addition, all the members of the National Council live outside our country, so we will build our own structure."'

Youssef rubs his eyelids: 'Delete "in the name of God" and the word "Arab".'

'But most of the people here are Arab, Syrian and Muslim.'

'Maybe, but there are also Kurds and Christians among us. That must be taken into account.'

'Qatar and Saudi Arabia will not support us if our words aren't Islamic in character.'

'It doesn't matter! The Syrians will support us everywhere, believe me. We don't need strangers to help us. We must remain independent—this is the foundation of freedom.'

Bilal stares at his cell phone, petrified, his eyes bulging.

'What's the matter?'

He remains silent.

'What is happening to you? Are you dead?

'Not me, Adel.'

32

The fruit seller is driving the taxi; Adel is slumped in the seat next to him. The bullet has struck one of his kidneys. 'Breathe, wake up.' His body seized with tremors, he collapses on the old man, uttering Sukayna's name. 'No, you are not going to die for me, I will not accept that!' They arrive at Homs Military Hospital.

The man carries Adel and runs to the emergency room, but it is already too late. The nurse who takes charge searches the pockets of the deceased and asks who killed him. The fruit seller tells him everything. He takes a step back: 'His head fell there', he points at his knee.

'I did what I could, he wasn't heavy, but I can't feel my legs any more. I can't walk. He's not dead, is he?'

'Go away! Get out!' the nurse told him.

'I came to this hospital because it is the closest, but you are just a bunch of criminals.'

The guards arrive, as the fruit seller continues:

'Look, in my whole life, I haven't hurt anyone, not even the donkey pulling my cart, not even the soldier who slapped me! But I'll kill you if you don't bring him back to life.'

The guards grab him, intent on throwing him out. Upon hearing the noise, a doctor comes out and asks the nurse what's going on.

'Another Opposition rat has died.'

33

For Youssef and Bilal, the most unbearable part is yet to come—informing Adel's wife Sukayna. What they don't know is that the hospital has already taken care of it: 'Come and pick up your husband's corpse,' the nurse said curtly before hanging up.

Sukayna remembers that on their wedding night, while lifting her muslin veil, Adel had whispered to her, 'No matter what the future holds, your name flows through me like my blood.'

Adel's lifeless body is lying on a gurney in one of the hospital's corridors; employees walk around it without paying any attention. The doctor lifts the sheet: 'Is that him?' She does not answer.

The hospital manager who asked to see her guides her to his office: 'This is what happens to those who hit our soldiers.' He places a sheet of paper in front of her on which is written: 'I, Sukayna, daughter of Abd al-Rahman, wife of the martyr Adel, hereby testifies that my husband was killed by a group of terrorists.' Sukayna stands, staring blankly, as the man hands her a pen: 'Anyway, you can't change the past. Sign here so that you can bury your husband. We know people like you too well. You are going to speak to the media and say that it was the al-Assad regime that killed him.'

She doesn't listen to him. She remembers the meal she left cooking on the stove. The little one is all alone at home. She needs to get back as soon as possible. Adel will not be long, and he will be hungry.

'As you wish. You don't sign, you don't get him back.' She complies, crying for the first time since hearing the news over the phone. Her tears mix with the ink. She faints.

34

From: Youssef <youssefcadi@gmail.com>

Sent: 07 November 2011

To: Mohammad <mohammadamir@gmail.com>

Subject: Following up on our first meeting

The best of our activists has been killed. His name was Adel and everyone loved him. We went to his house to wash his body and wrap him in a shroud. His face was serene, he even looked happy!

Many people gathered outside the front door. We carried him on our shoulders, through the middle of the crowd.

'Allah Akbar! God is great!' The crowd kept repeating, and everyone wanted to carry the coffin. When we arrived at the square, more than two thousand people were waiting for us. We circled the square three times. It was like a protest that did not want to end. Some waved the Islamic State flag and suddenly I heard someone shout: 'The people want jihad.'

The Syrians are angry and desperate. They can think of nothing but revenge. Faced with this state-sponsored violence, they seek ways to save themselves, even if it comes from Heaven.

But they don't realize the risk this slogan and what stands behind it represent.

When Adel was put in the ground, a man pulled out a gun and shot in the air. I shouted at him: 'Are you crazy? Stop!' But he continued and others did the same, shouting, 'Adel's blood is worth that of a hundred regime supporters!'

Unable to do anything, even the ground vibrated along with their voices. No one had any authority any more, nor could anyone be heard. Without Adel, we are all orphans, everyone on their own.

I came home with tremendous energy, as if I could move mountains. Sometimes losing a loved one makes us stronger.

I got used to the spectacle of death. The first time I saw a corpse, I had nightmares for a week. My neighbours brought home a man who had been shot in the back of the head. His neck was covered in blood. Someone shouted, 'Film, film this! Everyone needs to know what's going on here! Film it!' I pulled out my camera. I couldn't believe he was really dead, that he wouldn't come back. Part of me was trying to convince myself that he was asleep and was going to wake up. One of his relatives was banging his head against the door. I felt dizzy and wanted to throw up. The blood stain gradually widened, soaking up his white shirt. The blood dripped onto the floor, onto my shoes. The man's face was turned towards me, towards the camera, he was looking at me. He spoke to me: 'Don't forget me, I left too soon . . .' I smelled the odour of death, a strange odour, unlike any other: it stays in my head, I smell it every time I remember the scene. I see the faces again, I hear the voices of the people present, and it all reminds me of that smell. Dozens of subsequent deaths have passed in front of my camera, but never again have I felt that way.

Being so close to violence makes me appreciate the simple things more: today I love music, flowers or taking a shower. And sometimes I dream of a butterfly half black with yellow spots, half white with brown spots. I have researched this specimen, it is rare: neither male nor female.

All I want right now is to lay my head on your chest and fall into a deep sleep.

35

Josephine walks quickly towards the Nofara Café. She has already postponed her meeting with Khalil several times. Organizing demonstrations has kept him busy in recent days. When she finds him, Khalil's shoulders are drooping, his face has paled. He takes off his glasses.

'My mother is ill. I can't go and see her in Daraa, the region is full of checkpoints that I won't be able to pass.'

'You want me to take you and smuggle you in?'

'I'm afraid for you, Josephine.'

'Did you forget I have a doctorate in smuggling?'

Khalil crosses his fingers on the table.

'In Daraa, it's different from here. The soldiers scrutinize people's faces, and you also have to go to Homs to formally offer your condolences to Adel's family.'

'Yesterday, when I watched his funeral on Al Jazeera and saw people calling for jihad, I thought to myself that the revolution was being slaughtered.'

They change the subject when the waiter arrives and order two cappuccinos. They wait for him to leave before resuming. Josephine moves back in her seat.

'The problem is, every time we want to do something, we get hit by a disaster. How could we ask the Syrians to unite when the Alawites killed Adel? How could we form the Opposition if activists are arrested every week? The international community is doing nothing either, in its eyes we are nothing but cockroaches.'

'Did you hear the UN secretary general's last speech?'

'Yes, he said he was worried about the situation in Syria. He repeated this over and over. We should send him anti-anxiety drugs!'

After leaving the cafe, they walk around and leave the old town. Khalil hesitates; he would like to tell her that she is the dearest person in the world to him.

'Come with me to Homs,' she suggests.

'I prefer to stay in Damascus. Here I'm closer to Daraa.'

As they reach Bab Sharqi, in a small alley, in front of a jasmine plant, he slowly draws closer to her. She smiles. She looks at him with pure eyes. He puts his hand on her waist. She doesn't move. He plants a kiss on her forehead, then on her lips. Confused, he pulls away. She catches him suddenly, their lips meet, he wraps his arms around her. Their fingers wander over each other's cheeks. A ray of light pierces the interlacing branches of a tree and illuminates their kiss.

With the tip of her index finger, Josephine brushes a mole on Khalil's neck, pausing, as if wanting an imprint of it on her skin. An unusual scene in Damascus, Syria, and the Middle East, but the two of them are far from all traditions, far from the present.

She pulls away from him and walks off, not without turning around one last time. Khalil finally feels like he's in the right place, that he has found the country he's been looking for since birth.

36

From: Mohammad <mohammadamir@gmail.com>

Sent: November 10, 2011

To: Youssef <youssefcadi@gmail.com>

Subject: Following up on our first meeting

What freedom is it you're fighting for? Political Islam is stronger than you think it is, and there's nothing we can do to stop it. All it would take to destroy the planet is for the king of Saudi Arabia to call on Muslims around the world to jihad. We're the heirs of our parents' and ancestors' failures. The fruit of archaic centuries.

Yesterday evening, below my apartment, a dozen people surrounded my neighbour, the informant. One of them threatened him, flashing a knife in his face:

'Tell the truth or we'll kill you!'

'I didn't touch the child! He's lying! I'm impotent!'

'That's exactly what the child said! It's just further proof that you're guilty! You have twenty-four hours to get out of the neighbourhood.'

The man had told the little boy that his mother was waiting for him in the courtyard of the building. After the boy followed him, the guy forced him to undress. Fortunately, the child's mother came out of her apartment and called the boy. The bastard had threatened to kill him if he revealed what had happened, but the kid fled down the stairs, screaming.

This story crushed me. I lay down on the sofa, I felt dizzy, I felt like the victim. When I was about his age, I walked into a grocery and the grocer asked me to help him bring up boxes of chocolates from the cellar, promising to give me a large piece. I went down cheerfully, but while I was looking for the boxes, the man closed the door, locking us both in. He then looked at me in a way I will never forget: he was a wolf before a lamb. I tried to run away but he tackled me facing the wall. Taking my hand, he forced me to touch his penis, explaining that it would be best for me to do what he wanted, then he would give me the chocolate. Trapped in his arms, I couldn't free myself. He rubbed against me until he got what he was looking for.

I have never had the courage to tell this story to anyone.

37

Khalil lives in northwest Damascus, at the end of Barza, in a room overlooking farms. He chose this quiet, isolated location so he could easily escape in the event of an intelligence raid.

This Thursday, as the sun goes down, people are quietly returning home after buying what they need for tomorrow, Friday, their day off. The younger set prepare for a long day of demonstrations, but the older people and children won't go out again until Saturday.

Khalil walks into a shop and tells the seller that the price of rice has doubled since last week.

'Look at the fruits and vegetables! Have you seen the prices? In a few months we'll be dreaming of these prices. Big brands hold back their products and it's almost impossible to import anything. Thank God we have agriculture, otherwise we'd starve.'

Khalil doesn't feel like arguing; he picks up his bag of groceries and leaves. The neighbourhood is very quiet, almost sad, and he can't wait to get home. He decides to call Josephine to tell her he will join her in Homs. He's happy, even though he feels guilty about leaving while his mother is sick.

As he puts his key in the lock, he tells himself he has to go to the barbershop before he leaves and that he should buy a present for Josephine. A hand from behind seizes him violently by the throat and chokes him. Two men blindfold and gag him.

38

From: Youssef <youssefcadi@gmail.com>

Sent: November 14, 2011

To: Mohammad <mohammadamir@gmail.com>

Subject: Following up on our first meeting

On Friday, a group of visitors comes to the Centre without warning. They arrive one after the other, and an hour later it's ten of them. People's lives have turned into total chaos, most no longer have jobs. Every day, a strike, a demonstration, or a massacre disrupts their daily lives.

Despite this, people are still alive and cross the Street of Death—so called because it's targeted by snipers—not knowing if they will reach the other side alive or if a bullet will pierce their heart or their head. But they have grown used to this uncertainty: their old way of life comes back to them like a scene from a movie. And if they get to the other side, they feel like they've been reborn.

Around lunchtime, everyone agrees that if we were in Tunisia, where the population is all Sunni, this war would not be taking place. No strife between religions and ethnicities there. Their army forced the president to flee. I wondered if the chicken we were devouring was Sunni or Alawite. I'm not joking: these days, most people's discussions revolve around this question.

At the day's end, there was only one old man left at the Centre; he was wearing a keffiyeh. I was a little embarrassed by his presence and pretended to be working on my computer. 'I lived through the 1973 war against Israel, the civil war in Lebanon, the events of the 1980s between the regime and the Muslim Brotherhood. Thousands of young people have been murdered, and look at me, I'm still alive! The war will pass, we are eternal. Don't worry too much, my little one!' he told me before a knock on the door interrupted him. The old man opened with a sigh: 'Oh my God! I told you I'd be back in ten minutes!'

'I told you not to be late!'

'I'm sorry.'

'I married you forty years ago, and you have never been on time!'

He touches the arm of the woman who entered the room.

'Yes, when we got engaged, I arrived there right on time.'

'No, you were half an hour early.'

'I missed you!'

'That was long ago . . .'

'If I were with you a million years and you slipped away for even one minute, I'd miss you more than anything.'

She laughs and claps.

He grabs her hand. She tries to pull it away, laughing. 'Stop, we're not at home!'

Before he leaves, the old man turns to me and says, 'I love it when she's mad at me. Afterwards, when she forgives me, her eyes are so beautiful!'

It's people like these who give me hope for the future. We are alive despite the ruins that surround us.

As for your neighbour and what resurfaced from your childhood after that episode, I know you will never be able to forget it. But be sure that I will carry this memory with you forever.

39

Weapons produce frightful noise when they strike metal objects. Khalil listens intently to everything he hears to determine where he has been taken. Cops lead him through hallways where dampness and the smell of mould mingle with that of blood. They take him down a long staircase before removing his blindfold and gag and pushing him into a cell where his head violently bashes against another inmate.

About twenty people are in this ten-square-metre room, half standing, the other half seated. The jailer yells, 'If I hear a word, I'll send you straight to the gallows!' Khalil needs someone to talk to, to make sure he's not having a nightmare. Despite the darkness, he can see a man of about sixty beside him, whip marks streaking his gaunt face. The man wears what appears to be a white shirt covered with grime and he breathes with difficulty. He explains to Khalil that they are in Faraa in Palestine. Dread grips Khalil: he's been taken to the regime's torture and death centre.

'Why are you here?' Khalil asks the man.

The prisoner scratches his lice-filled hair before replying, 'My son took part in the protests and the police want him to surrender. They are using me to put pressure on him.'

'And the others?'

'They are all here for political reasons.'

In one corner, a teenage boy lies restless on the ground, blood flowing from his mouth and staining his clothes. The other inmates try to calm him down and get him to drink some water, but the boy keeps moaning. His legs are covered with cigarette burns.

Sitting in a corner, Khalil dozes off and wakes up with a start. The man says to him: 'You're still new, you'll get used to sleeping sitting up.'

40

'Now that Adel is gone, who is going to protect us?' Youssef's tears roll down into Josephine's hair. She squeezes his shoulders gently: 'I don't want to hear this talk of despair. We still have a lot of work to do. I have a new project for the end of the year. We are going to bring gifts to the neighbourhood children! We'll sing and dance with them, despite everything.'

After the tragedy, Adel's wife went to live with her family; she didn't want to run into anyone from the Centre. At her husband's burial, she just scooped up some dirt in her hand and squeezed it with all her might, then left alone and in silence. Nothing could have soothed her grief; her pain was greater than anything imaginable.

'That's natural, she lost her husband, and the authorities won't let her denounce his killer.'

Josephine gives Youssef the bag of medicines she brought: 'Get them quickly to the nurse. I'm exhausted. We should cook something to eat.' But a call from Rachid brings them back to a harsh reality: 'Khalil was taken on a trip—be careful!'

41

From: Mohammad <mohammadamir@gmail.com>

Sent: November 21, 2011

To: Youssef <youssefcadi@gmail.com>

Subject: Following up on our first meeting

If I hadn't hung around today, I would have died.

I left the Chez Nous restaurant around noon. I then strolled through the surrounding streets, heading for Qassaa Street. Ten minutes before I got there, a shell, launched from Douma, exploded there. I ran to the impact site where many people were already gathered.

Here's a weird thing about this country: when you hear a warplane or a helicopter, you go out on your patio to watch rather than go down to the cellar to protect yourself. And when an attack occurs, we rush to the place when we should get away from it. No one ever runs away.

At least seven people were killed today. I wondered which victim had died instead of me. The police quickly closed the street. Heavy smoke blanketed everything, flames rose from a butcher's shop, and a car was completely destroyed. Doctors identified the wounded who were then loaded into ambulances. I couldn't see everything that was going on, I was too far away.

A woman arrived screaming, 'My mother! My mother!' I was in shock, not just at this horrific scene, but at the thought that the militias in Douma might have known that the bomb would fall on civilians. Muslims or Christians. For or against the regime.

I continued walking and arrived at Sebki Garden. There were no leaves on the trees any more, and their branches seemed to sag more than usual. Was it because of this ageing city or the weight of what we were going through? In the garden, a family: a mother, a father and their two children, all lying in the grass on beds of cardboard. In the past, people loved to bask in nature; now they stay there. This family lives in the garden, like other displaced people in Damascus. They fled the violence of war only to reach the hell of cold and beggary.

I didn't want to go to work. I was depressed that people had run out of money to buy food . . .

When I was little, I would take meat from the fridge at home and plant it in the orchard. I imagined it would grow and become a sheep tree, so no one would go hungry anymore. Now I wish I could do the same with fabric and give people clothes they can no longer afford.

When I got to al-Halbouni, my favourite neighbourhood, hundreds of books were strewn on the pavements. It's a wonderful thing in this neighbourhood. Vendors of used and antique books protect them with large umbrellas; some even go home to rest leaving the books unattended, because they are sure thieves will not be interested in reading. Not far from them, on the other side of the street, a vendor offered all kinds of items: Coke, chewing gum, bracelets, combs, etc., all at one hundred pounds. A little boy and a little girl approached him:

'We only have fifty pounds, can we buy half a bracelet?' The man told them to go away without even looking at them.

'Please! I promised my sister I would buy her a present. Look, her arm is very small, half a bracelet will do.'

I bought the children what they wanted. Their joy in that moment was more important to me than the revolution, the victory and everything in-between.

42

The jailer slams the cell door open and places a bucket and a plate of dry bread and olives on the floor: 'The pig's breakfast is served! Where's the last asshole we took? Come on, the chief wants to see you!'

He grabs Khalil by the neck and drags him towards the interrogation room. The officer sits at a desk, reading documents spread out in front of him while smoking and drinking his coffee. 'Khalil al-Musaddi, twenty-four, chemistry student, born in Daraa, resident in Damascus, member of Daou, an Opposition group,' he says loudly. The office is richly decorated. The table is of fine wood; a gold pistol and antiques rest on it. The sofas look comfortable, and a bookshelf contains a wealth of files alongside a large portrait of Bashar al-Assad. Written below it in capital letters: YES, A THOUSAND TIMES YES TO YOU, THE LEADER OF THE MOTHERLAND.

The buttons on the officer's uniform are about to pop from the pressure of his huge belly. He scrutinizes his prisoner for a long time.

'I know you're an intellectual, a smart man, and that's why you're going to help me. I only have one question—if you answer it, you can go free. Who is with you in this group?'

Then, without waiting for a response, he adds, 'Did one of the guards hit you? If so, we're sorry but, you know, the country is at war . . .'

When he was arrested, Khalil was prepared to claim that he had no ties to political movements, but after his night in the cell he decided to change his position: he has nothing more to lose, he knows that they will hit him like the others. 'Mr Officer, I admit that I campaigned against the power in place, but believe me, I did nothing wrong.'

'I know you participated in the revolution in the North.'

'That's not true!'

'What?'

'I've never been to the North!'

'That means you've demonstrated elsewhere, but that's not what interests me. I want to know why.'

'To free political detainees, for democracy and for independent, impartial justice.'

'And have you thought of Israel? Don't you know they're waiting for the first chance to pounce on us because of our support for the Palestinians? Are you not aware there is a plot against Syria?'

Khalil has a bad headache; he feels like his head is about to explode, every cell in his body hurts. 'Maybe, but what does this have to do with our demands?'

'Our enemies are on the prowl, they want to take advantage of the chaos to invade us. You only have to look at the map of the New Middle East to see it—the US Secretary of State Condoleezza Rice has been talking about it for years.'

He turns the screen of his computer towards Khalil so that he can see Syria divided into several micro-states: Damascus, Aleppo, the Alawites . . .

'I know that, and I oppose this plan.'

'Fool! You support it by creating this mess you call the revolution! Do you want to bring down the regime? What did it do to you? You have forgotten its benefits: schools, universities and hospitals are all free. Our country is self-sufficient in food, which is available everywhere. You live in safety thanks to us. What more do you want?'

He continues: 'You are like a naked man searching for a tie. We are a developing country, let's eradicate illiteracy first, we'll talk about freedom later.'

'Why didn't you listen to us at the start? We did not want to overthrow the regime, but to set up a real parliament and live with dignity.'

'It takes time, a lot of time. Today, Syria is in danger . . .'

'It's because of you!'

'No, from you who continue your activities against the authorities. Anyway, tell me, who is with you in this group?'

'I don't know what group you're talking about.'

Khalil asks for a sip of water, but the officer speaks as if he can't hear.

'Don't be afraid, I just want to contact them to make a deal. Al-Qaida has entered the territory, in the eastern regions, and the Muslim Brotherhood is ready to act. They want to establish an Islamic state. Would that make you happy? No? So, tell me who was with you!'

'I've always been alone.'

The officer throws his cigarette at the young man: 'Alone. Here too you are alone.' He rings a doorbell behind his desk and immediately a guard enters: 'Take him away and keep an eye on him!'

Moments later, Khalil is standing, barefoot, in a small room with a metal floor. An electric shock passes through his body. He jumps, runs and yells: 'Stop! I will confess, I will confess!' Everything revolves around him, his feet are scorched, on fire, his eyesight blurs, he sees only black, no longer feels his hands, no longer has the strength to cry out.

43

Ever since learning the news, Josephine stays glued to her laptop, constantly looking out for any bit of information. Without warning, Youssef slams the laptop shut.

'Why are you doing this? I was sending an email. You're driving me crazy!'

'You need to rest a little.'

'You don't know how guilty I feel. I told him he would come here with me. Our last date had changed my life.'

She throws herself on the locked door and bangs angrily. 'I want to be in jail with him, I can't wait any longer!'

Youssef, who followed her, takes her hands in his: 'Stop, he'll come out of prison, I'm sure.'

He sits down and puts on some music—Chopin's Nocturnes—then goes to make her a cup of chamomile. An hour passes in silence before Bilal arrives.

'They're setting us up one by one like rabbits and won't stop until they've had the last one!'

'Khalil's name was sent to Amnesty International, and a Facebook page created to demand his release. We must now start working on the constitution of the National Council that we want to put in place.'

'I'm not convinced by all of this any more . . . For now, we must find new allies, whoever they are. The most important thing right now is to be strong.'

Bilal angrily devours his meal at full speed, as if getting revenge on his diet.

Josephine's thoughts are on Khalil. She knows he has never liked living with others and wonders if he is in a collective or individual cell, what he thinks about, and whether he is being beaten. She looks up at the ceiling and sobs in silence.

44

'The people of Lot lived in the Arabian Peninsula some ten thousand years ago. God sent them a prophet so that they stop their sexual practices. As they ignored him, the angel Gabriel lifted the city up to Heaven before throwing it to the ground.'

Every morning as he gets dressed, Mohammad thinks about this text he studied in the mosque as a young man: 'Homosexuality existed among the Greeks. In *The Iliad* we discover the intimate relations between Achilles and Patroclus. These people weren't doing anything different from what I'm doing today. Why did this practice become a crime?' He asks himself.

He tries not to think about it any more. The first hour of the day is always very hard for him; sadness fills his heart and makes him want to cry.

But as he combs his hair, his mind drifts again. He thinks of the ancient Egyptians: 'Inside the pyramids, there are hieroglyphics in which men kiss each other. It's true that

I have not found stories about homosexuality among Arabs from before Islam. However, if the Prophet forbade it, it is proof that it existed.'

He puts the comb back in the cabinet to the right of his razor, closes the door, then opens it again and moves the comb to the left of the razor. He feels that if he had left it on the right, he would have had a problem today. He repeats this action three more times: he takes it, puts it back, checks that it is in its place and not crooked. If he wants to avoid running into people, he must leave right away. He doesn't want to be insulted while walking. But he still has to check that the bed sheet is pulled tight, so he retraces his steps and finds that everything is in order. Finally, he walks to the door, turns his head to make sure he hasn't forgotten anything, and quickly leaves.

When he arrives at Chez Nous, the spectacle that the city offers him improves his mood. He drinks his coffee while reading Youssef's emails. He starts his day full of energy.

45

When the torturers reconnect the power, Khalil's body shakes, which makes them laugh and say, 'The bastard is still alive.' One of them runs a finger along Khalil's cheek, 'Do you want to have some more fun, kid?'

The beefiest of them is over six feet tall, swinging his left arm while his right hand stays close to his pistol. He's one-eyed, having lost the other in a brawl, a cash game with colleagues that went wrong and ended in a stabbing. He is known as Dracula and is said to be the most experienced of all in the field of torture.

Without a word, he stretches Khalil's legs, grabs him by the neck and pushes his face to his knees. Bending him thus, he forces Khalil to slip into a tyre. He has fun spinning him around the room. At this point, Khalil wishes to die. The others laugh and encourage Dracula to continue.

Back in the cell, the prisoners help him lie down and try to feed him some leftover potatoes. Although his stomach is empty, the taste of potatoes makes him nauseous.

'Did you confess?' They ask him. Khalil shakes his head painfully in negation. 'Good! If you give them just one piece of information, they won't let you go.'

'How long have I been here?'

'Only three days.'

Khalil repeats this number to himself so as not to forget it.

'It is the torture sessions and the meals that punctuate our lives now.'

Long moments pass, moments during which silence envelops the prison. Khalil is still lying down. When the door opens again, diffusing fear into the room, everyone wonders, who will be next? Who is going to be tortured? Who is going to die?

And when it's time to go to the bathroom, they all run out, heads down, towards a four-foot square room at the end of the hall. Khalil drags himself there with difficulty and receives a whiplash. Once there, he can no longer move his feet. The jailer, annoyed, pulls him away by his hair.

'The minute has already passed, you piece of shit.'

46

From: Youssef <youssefcadi@gmail.com>
Sent: November 30, 2011
To: Mohammad <mohammadamir@gmail.com>
Subject: Following up on our first meeting

It is not only in Damascus that people sleep outside—in Homs too, but underground. There is no more room in cemeteries to bury our dead.

This city has always been nicknamed 'the mother of the poor'. The farmers continue their work, bringing their crops to the souks—nothing disturbs them, apart from the checkpoints where they barter some of their produce in exchange for their passage. Although clashes take place during the day, residents go out to buy food for their children. They use humour to confront the regime, the Opposition and themselves.

When the protests were broadcast live on satellite channels, everyone laughed, 'Why are there no longer people at the gatherings in Homs? Because the demonstrators stay at home hoping to see each other on TV!'

On the one hand, military reinforcements keep arriving; on the other, armed Islamist groups film themselves brandishing Kalashnikovs and then post the videos on YouTube. In Saudi Arabia, a donation campaign was launched in favour of the latter to finance the sending of weapons and money. Defenders of neighbourhoods that did not accept to be under their flag were driven out. These people who take up arms in the name of God are just as harmful and oppressive as the regime.

Last week, for example, an armoured vehicle crossed the main road in front of al-Khaldiya, showering the neighbourhood with bullets. Hiding behind a vehicle, I pulled out my camera as a man equipped with a grenade launcher moved to my side and got into position to open fire as well.

'What are you doing? You're filming us, you traitor!' One of his comrades threatened me with a pistol. He took me to their base so they could inspect my videos and, finding no image of the man with the RPG, they let me go. The next day, they sent an emissary who told me, 'You must have our authorization to film, otherwise you will be sentenced to death.'

After Adel's death, dozens of leaders emerged in the area, each claiming to be better than their neighbour and wanting to lead the revolution. I feel like a stranger in my own neighbourhood.

47

Before the war, when people met in the Old Town of Homs, it was in front of a particular shop or restaurant. But since the army entered the city, the landmarks have changed. When Rachid arrives in al-Khaldiya, he follows Youssef's directions: 'Continue to a small crossroads. Turn left where there are bullet holes on a *mashrabiyah*. Continue straight ahead until you reach the collapsed wall. I'll meet you there.'

At the Centre, Youssef blocks the door to the room that serves as the dispensary so Rachid cannot see the child with a shoulder injury in there. The kid was playing football with his friends; when the ball rolled towards the main road and he ran to catch it, a sniper hit him.

Josephine is wrapped in a blanket. Firewood supplies are late today. 'Why have you come this far? Travelling has become very dangerous these days.'

'I'm here to say goodbye to you.'

'Are you leaving for Mars?'

'No, for Turkey. I've made up my mind. No. It's not a decision, it's an obligation. I do not have a choice. I have to flee, that's all. My relatives on the coast threatened me after they saw me on TV participating in a protest. They said they were going to find me and slit my throat.'

'But what are you going to do in Erdogan's country?'

'It doesn't matter. I'll sweep the streets, sell newspapers. I have friends there who will help me. I just want to get out of this horror. It's not only those close to me that I'm worried about, but also the prospect of ending up in prison. As long as Khalil was around, I felt strong. Ever since they arrested him, I have had nightmares every night. I have visions of soldiers torturing me and giving me electric shocks.'

Josephine puts her hand on his arm: 'Don't worry, you're safe here. The electricity is often cut off and even when it's available, it's very weak.'

'I'm not kidding. You know very well that the Alawites who support the revolution are considered double traitors. We should be on the side of Bashar, who is "one of us". I can't bear the idea of being in prison. Even when I was little, the hardest thing was when my father forbade me from leaving the house. It was horrible. How do you think I'd survive in a small cell? I would end up going crazy.'

The wood finally arrives and Youssef lights the stove: 'See, the trees are also victims of this war, since fuel is so expensive.' He cleans his hands with a tissue. Josephine throws back her blanket; she's wearing jeans and a black sweater.

'Black looks good on you, princess,' Rachid tells her after looking at her.

'Thank you, my king. Do you have everything ready for your trip?'

'I know a guy from Aleppo who's in contact with a truck driver. He's the one who will take me across the border. At the checkpoint, I'll say I'm his assistant. I feel sad about leaving our country this way, but hey . . .'

He brushes a fly off his pants.

'After all we've lost, nothing in this country deserves our sadness.'

'We are still here—if you stay, you won't be alone.'

'We're the same, my dear, cornered between the regime and the Islamists.'

He sits up, his lips twitch, his face darkens.

'I'm leaving tomorrow. Can I sleep here tonight?'

'No, you can't. We'll let you sleep in the street,' smiles Josephine.

'That's nice. I have a bottle of arak—we're going to drink it.'

'You're going to miss it.'

'Do you think I haven't thought about that? Arak comes from Greece, it went through Turkey before coming to us. I am just getting closer to the source of this sacred drink.'

His eyes light up.

'They don't make it the same way, but I'll manage. Maybe I'll work in a wine cellar. That was my project for ages: to make alcohol. It's like remaking the world—it never dies; instead, it gets younger over time. It's magic.'

48

From: Mohammad <mohammadamir@gmail.com>

Sent: December 04, 2011

To: Youssef <youssefcadi@gmail.com>

Subject: Following up on our first meeting

In 1958, when Shukri al-Quwatli ceded power to Gamal Abdel Nasser, after they had decided to unite Egypt and Syria into one state, he declared, 'I give you a people who are half prophets and half leaders. I have understood this for years. You, on the other hand, are obstinate. You want to change society when all I want is for nothing to change.'

I read a text that reminded me of you: 'During the invasion of Iraq, one of Muhammad's companions, Khaled Ibn al-Walid, met an effeminate young man. He informed the caliph, who ordered him to burn this young man.' Khaled would come out of his grave that's near you in al-Khaldiya if he knew your and my history. We're going to end up in the fire.

I am writing to you from the Café Rawda. From my seat I can see the Parliament. You told me you love this building but hate the people in it. I'm not surprised that you like it, since it was built by the French. Thanks to you, I read up on the subject and was surprised to learn that the plan of the capital was drawn up by them. They built the town hall of Marjeh, the Hospital for Foreigners and several neighbourhoods in Damascus, including Qassaa.

French Damascus, your sweetheart, wants to see you. When will you come to visit?

The girls here are charming, and the boys beautiful. They walk hand in hand—and no one is paying attention to me. I am alone. My days pass, filled with your absence, my sadness and the books I read.

49

The officer makes a pretence of asking Khalil if his jailers tortured him. 'The bastards, I told them to watch out for you! Anyway, don't lose hope, I saw your name on the news. You're famous, well done!'

He brings his face towards Khalil's until they almost touch: 'To your comrades you may be a hero, but in reality you're nothing but a traitor. You must understand we're the ones who have the power. You're nothing. We can crush you in a matter of days. You're lucky we're being soft with you.'

He returns to his desk and pulls out an empty whiskey bottle. 'I drank it yesterday, but kept the bottle because we might need it later—unless you need to prove your loyalty to your homeland.' Fear leaves Khalil's face, a volcano of anger awakens in him. He smiles at the officer.

'Give me the names of those who are with you.'

'It is a group of men and women who reject oppression and dictatorship.'

The officer calls two guards, orders them to lay Khalil on his stomach and hold him tight. They take off his pants and the officer shoves the bottle in his anus: 'Are you having a good time? Is that how the Islamists fuck you? Or are there other positions?'

Khalil weeps in pain and his cry echoes between the walls of the prison.

'Say: "I am a donkey!"'

He clenches his jaws but receives a blow on the mouth.

'When I ask you to do something, you do it!' Say: "I am a donkey!"'

'I am a donkey.'

'I'm a whore!'

'I'm a whore.'

'I suck your cocks!'

'I suck your cocks.'

'Bashar is my God!'

'Bashar is my God.'

'See how nice this boy is!'

'He is so obedient.'

Eventually the officer removes the bottle and immediately blood begins to run down Khalil's thighs. He grits his teeth.

The three henchmen turn him over onto his back and put his feet up for the officer to whip them.

The blows rain down. 'And now? Are you still strong? Do you still want to play the rebel?' The prisoner's skin is shredded. The torturer's hand hurts, he throws the whip to the ground. 'Take him to cell number 4. Be careful, I don't want him to die.'

50

From: Youssef <youssefcadi@gmail.com>

Sent: December 12, 2011

To: Mohammad <mohammadamir@gmail.com>

Subject: Following up on our first meeting

You live through the eyes of others as if you existed only through them. You'd like to be like them. Truth is, even if you had friends, you'd remain isolated. Your loneliness is within you, it inhabits you.

Here, around me, I only see the wounded, the killed, the killers or the survivors seeking revenge. The other day I greeted a group of young men from Deir Baalbah. Do you know this town? Most of its inhabitants are Bedouin who support the Opposition. Residents of Abbassiya, a pro-regime Shiite neighbourhood, kidnapped some of their children and slaughtered them before dumping the bodies on the main road. These young people, whom I met, wanted to trap a car in this lair of murderers. I asked them how they planned to protect civilians.

'All assassins,' they replied.

They wanted me to help them transport the vehicle, but I refused. They are savages and we don't have to follow their example. The only victory in this war is in keeping our humanity.

The French aspect of Damascus will perhaps disappear during this revolution as it did in Homs. We only borrowed architecture from France; we should also have studied their language and benefited from their experience in the field of human rights. But the 'anti-imperialist' regime prevented us from doing so.

All that remains of French culture now are the words 'pâtisserie' or 'boulangerie', written in the Arabic alphabet in some neighbourhoods. Even your favourite restaurant, Chez Nous, doesn't mean anything to most customers. They pronounce it 'Shey no'. Just like the La vache qui rit cheese: 'La vashkri'. I also miss the Moulin Rouge—did you know it's a French name? In Paris, it's not a nightclub like here; it's a cabaret, a room that presents revues.

I am writing to you in front of the wood stove. I really like its flame. Impossible to look away from it. What is the origin of this fire? What tree does it come from? And what will become of it tomorrow? Voices of insurgents? Clouds?

51

Dracula comes to get the old man; he pulls him by his feet: 'I'm going to hang you upside down for three days!' The man moaned.

'Do anything you want, but not that! The other time, I thought my head was going to explode.' He tries to resist; his shirt is half torn.

'Please, you are my son's age, I know you are a good person!' He extends his hand to his executioner as if to shake his.

The jailer freezes and orders him to repeat what he just said. 'I could be your father.'

He grabs the prisoner's head and bangs it against a metal column. 'You bastard! You—my father? You? You?' The man does not move. His skull is shattered. 'Throw that trash away,' Dracula yells at the guards.

One of the guards loads the corpse onto a truck and, like every day, goes to a secret location and gets rid of his cargo.

Khalil witnesses the whole scene from his new cell where he is now alone. At this moment, all he thinks of is suicide in this bare-walled room. To do that, he would have to reach a small opening into which he could put his head and hang himself. The problem is his hands, which would reflexively grip the walls to keep him from dying.

He thinks of his mother. The last time he saw her, she gave him a blue sweater that she had knit herself. He was wearing it when he was arrested. His mother's perfume envelops him despite the smell of blood. He wonders if she's still alive and if she knows where he is. He wants to break everything, but his numb muscles and swollen feet bring him back to the present. A joke that people make when they want to criticize the government comes to mind 'What's your shoe size? It will soon change.'

In the evening, he lies on his side. To console himself, he imagines being in a cafe with Josephine. She takes his hand and kisses it. Outside there is a Christmas tree. At this very moment, Damascus must be illuminated by lights of all colours; the Old City must be invaded by children and their mothers, especially the al-Hamidiyah souk. Khalil has never liked shopping, but there he sees a pink dress adorned with white butterflies. He buys it for Josephine. They're going to spend the evening at his place; he has lit candles and brought out red wine. Josephine is wearing his present to her, a dress that bares half of her back. It fits her perfectly, as if it had been made for her. He desires every part of her body. He waits for the passion to peak, like a full moon.

The shadow of Josephine's cigarette stretches into her half-full glass. She talks about the coast, where she was born and raised. 'There, people are like waves: suddenly they get angry, insult you for no reason and then hug you.' She tells him that every morning she would wait for the geese and feed them. Khalil kisses her. He tastes her lips. She tries to hide her blush by laughing.

Will he ever be able to make love to her? He was repeatedly punched on the genitals and on the testicles. The men would say to him: 'We're going to fuck your sisters in front of you soon!'

Is it true?

He doesn't know, but what he is sure of is that Beethoven's music fills his house as he explains to the woman he loves why he chose to study chemistry: 'I love it when the elements react. In high school, I had a small room with a terrace where I carried out experiments to invent a new colour. Today, I do the same with love: chemistry is the basis.'

He decides to recite to her a poem he wrote a long time ago; he feels that this is the best moment:

In the forest of our bodies
Our feet entwined between two skies
Half of me is in the light
The other flies in your breath

You guide me to my face
To the wind, and the alphabet

If there is home
It's when I forget the killers' season
In this light that rises from your voice

52

Josephine wakes up with puffy eyes. She has no energy, but at the thought of Khalil she jumps off the mattress and opens the window. The cold dashes through the room like an arrow.

As she walks to the bathroom, she hears Bilal arriving at the Centre. A strange feeling has begun to grow inside her since the last time he came. He didn't look at her during their discussion, he was even avoiding her eyes. 'The heads of the neighbourhood may not agree, Christmas is a Christian custom, it is not welcome in Islam,' Bilal told Youssef.

Josephine replies, 'You mean the Islamists in the neighbourhood? Saudi Arabia–backed militias? Just say it.'

He pretends he's too busy with his cell phone to hear her.

'Why don't you talk to me any more, Bilal?'

'OK, OK! All right: the Islamists.'

'I know you can't protest without their consent, but it's not their city. What gives them the right to control us? Money and guns? Who are these idiots? What do they want? An Islamic state? Look at me. I am a free woman. I don't want to bring down the regime just to have new dictators who'll force women to wear the veil.'

Bilal sighs, 'Let me be honest. I don't work with you alone. I made a deal with the Muslim Brotherhood. They gave me cameras and money.'

Youssef hangs his jacket on the coat rack.

'In exchange for what?'

'In exchange for raising in the demonstrations banners that support the National Council. I'm on their side. We lose nothing by saying we're on their side. Then we'll do whatever we want.'

'You can't do as you please any more. You already owe them.'

'We have no other choice.'

'Of course we do! We can continue our fight.'

'And do what? Give gifts to children?'

'We have to go out and protest and you have to be with us! We want families to gather in the square. We will sing and celebrate. A friend will bring us gifts and clothes from Damascus.'

'Inshallah,' Bilal said as he left.

Josephine closes the window as sadness sets in. Only weeks earlier, this young man had been their comrade. Now everything has changed, and she feels like she never even knew him. She waits for Youssef to speak, but he remains silent. She asks him what he thinks about all this. 'I don't have time to think. The main thing is to continue our work.' A large black cloud covers the sky. 'We are really alone, very alone. Why doesn't anyone care about us? Our victims have become mere numbers in the news.'

'Did we save the Romanians when Ceauşescu crushed them? Or the Iraqis when George Bush bombed them? Why would the others be on our side? Massacres are now part of everyday life here. In Europe, it's the end-of-the-year celebrations, they're having fun on vacation. We did nothing when the children of Somalia were starving. I once read a play where a man has a conversation with a tiger. "We killed ten million people in the Second World War." The animal replies, "And you ate them all?" The man cries out, "No!" The beast is surprised: "So why did you kill them?"'

53

From: Mohammad <mohammadamir@gmail.com>

Sent: December 18, 2011

To: Youssef <youssefcadi@gmail.com>

Subject: Following up on our first meeting

From my bedroom I can see an apartment in the building across the street. Every night, a woman in her fifties takes some clothes out of a closet: a red skirt and a white T-shirt, puts them on the bed and sits next to them. She talks to them for an hour. I'd like to know her secret: has she lost someone and gone mad with loneliness? This kind of behaviour is no longer strange in Damascus—many locals are soliloquists. I have already met several people like this on the street. Before, we used to call them crazy. Now it's become normal.

To change the opinion of the people in my neighbourhood about me, I brought a prostitute to my house. Before going upstairs, we stood in front of my building for a while so that my neighbours could see us.

I put my sex inside her. I felt nothing. I no longer had an erection. I withdrew and lay down, like a defeated soldier. She said,

'Don't worry, now most men are like you. It's the depression, the fear. You sleep with women as if you were fighting a war. It has debased you.'

I told her I wasn't like the others, and she laughed, 'You all say the same thing! I know you very well, against or with the regime, military or civilian, worker or minister, you are defeated everywhere, even in the sack.'

She gave me some Viagra and said that even young people were taking it now. I refused. She kissed me on the forehead, took her money and left.

An hour later, I heard the voice of the imam reciting a Quranic verse about paradise: 'And among them, boys will circulate eternally young. When you see them, you will take them for scattered pearls.' I imagined around me rivers, trees, bunches of grapes, castles made of gold bricks, a very handsome teenager passing by . . . what a perversion! For centuries, millions of people have believed this.

This is the story we learnt at school, at home, at university.

But I don't care about all that: my problem today is to know if I'm normal.

54

From: Youssef <youssefcadi@gmail.com>

Sent: 19 December 2011

To: Mohammad <mohammadamir@gmail.com>

Subject: Following up on our first meeting

We cherish our past because our present is painful, and we have lost our future. We are proud to have invented the number zero and to have offered it to the world. The problem is that we have not gone beyond that.

In Homs, prostitution exists but in a roundabout way: the remarriage of widows. When a woman loses her husband, she becomes by force of circumstance the second or even the third wife of a man who then becomes financially responsible for her. But for these men, the only motivation for marrying them is sex. They even strut around with guns as if they were their dicks.

I believe that if we were sexually free, if every man and woman could live their passions, war would end. No one would want to kill anyone any more. Drowned in desire, violence becomes an empty idea.

For my part, I'm convinced that my desire is intense, stronger than that of a straight man. Because sleeping with someone of the same sex means sleeping with a body that you know and understand.

Are you normal? Nothing is less important. Just see that you have the possibility to take on different roles in your fantasies, and when you have sex. Two boys. Two girls. A girl and a boy. On the other hand, in this ridiculous paradise that we are promised, I know that I will never be able to enjoy myself. If I die a martyr, I'll have to live with seventy-two virgins—what a nightmare!

You know what? Stop thinking about this crap and live a little! Get out of your depression! And if you meet someone who talks to themselves, talk to them!

A few days ago, a shell fell on al-Khaldiya but didn't explode. Some children played with it—they placed it on a swing strung to a tree, and swayed it back and forth while singing. This is our life!

55

They put Khalil back in the collective cell. There are fewer fellow prisoners now. The teenager in particular is no longer there.

'The guards made him swallow large amounts of salt and drink a lot of water. They also tightened a wire very firmly around his genitals and bound his hands and feet,' explains a young man sitting next to him. He wipes his eyes with his sleeve.

'He spent the night saying he was going to die here if this continued, and that he was willing to do anything they wanted to be released. The poor guy was writhing in pain. A few hours later, his bladder exploded.'

'The assho . . .' Khalil begins angrily, but the man stops him from finishing by placing his palm on his lips.

'I have nothing to do with anything that happened here. I am a computer scientist. Four years ago, I got a scholarship to the United States. I went, and later started working there too.'

'And then?'

'I came home last summer for vacation. I didn't really understand what was going on in the country. I didn't feel concerned, to tell you the truth.'

The young man tilts his head to the right and, despite his fatigue, expresses great gentleness.

'One Friday, when I went out of my parents' house to buy bread, I heard people shouting slogans in a nearby street. I approached out of curiosity. I found it interesting what they were saying, I liked it: "Freedom, pacifism, equality!" It was beautiful, exciting. Then the sound of bullets rang out. A group of police officers attacked the procession, and they took me away with them. That's how I ended up here. I am accused of having looked at the traitors with a smile.'

'Did they torture you?'

'Not a lot, compared with others. I was only given electric shocks and whipped. I've been here for five months now, not sure if they still remember me. I haven't been questioned for weeks . . . But I swear, I'm not an activist! I'm not involved in any political activity. I spend my life in front of my computer. If I leave my home, it's to go shopping or to a rock party. I play rock music, I even got an award in Los Angeles!'

The door opens and the jailer throws the prisoners' lunch on the floor, 'Bon appétit, you bunch of animals!'

The computer scientist doesn't move, so Khalil hands him a piece of potato.

'No thanks, my mom is expecting me for lunch, and I haven't brought the bread yet.'

'Mine is sick. That doesn't mean we have to stop living.'

The young man stares at Khalil, grabs the piece of potato and bites into it.

'You look a lot like my fiancée's brother.'

'Don't worry, you'll get out and see them again. They arrested me a few hours after I kissed the girl I love for the first time.'

'The intelligence services are very religious and a lot into Islamic morality.'

The young man laughs; Khalil notices he has a broken tooth. 'I lost it when they arrested me. A rifle butt. The soldier said to me, "This is so you will smile well the next time you see those bastards." Imagine, my tooth fell to the ground, it wasn't arrested. It's always free! Maybe the government is looking for it . . .'

In a cell next door, torture is taking place; the echoing sounds distress him, but the young man continues: 'I met my beloved here in Syria during the holidays. I wanted to go back to the United States with her. Our apartment there is ready. I decorated it well, with reproductions of paintings on the wall, especially Van Goghs that I love. There is also a large mirror and a rocking chair, so that if my wife is sitting there, I can look at her, either directly or in the mirror, no matter where I am in the living room. I bought a double bed, for the bedroom, with red pillows, very soft. I

145

was looking forward to the moment when we would begin this new life together. But since my arrest, I don't know if she's met anyone else or even if she's in jail like me.'

The two men then make an agreement: they exchange their addresses; the first to get out of this prison will tell the other's family that their son is still alive and where he is.

56

From: Mohammad <mohammadamir@gmail.com>

Sent: 23 December 2011

To: Youssef <youssefcadi@gmail.com>

Subject: Following up on our first meeting

I visited my father and I shouldn't have. He knew everything that happened to Sarah, but he didn't tell me so as not to hurt me: in Douma, she continued to work for the law firm. She sent the tally of victims during the demonstrations to human rights organizations. One of the local Islamist groups was unhappy with her activity over which they had no control. The building where Sarah works was attacked and everyone was arrested. Sarah's family got to know of all this through acquaintances. Sarah's kidnappers, after much negotiation, agreed to release her in exchange for 20,000 US dollars. Her parents had to sell their house to raise the money.

Since her release, her family has not let her out of the house. Her parents have let my dad know that the engagement is over because they think I'm the wrong man. Eventually, Sarah was forced to marry her cousin.

My dad has aged by twenty years lately. I tried to reassure him by pretending that everything was OK and everything would be fine at work. But I cannot hide the situation in the souk from a man who has spent his life in commerce. He said to me, 'No one makes any money and it will be even harder in the future. I'm going to sell the shop.' I begged him to change his mind. It took years of hard work for him to buy it. He refused—he's stubborn as a mule, like you.

My father was lying down and was coughing very hard again. He didn't want me to call a doctor. I promised him that I'd get married very soon and that he'd be able to see his grandchildren playing around him. He silenced me with a wave of his hand, 'I heard bad things about you. Tell me, is that right—are you sleeping with homosexuals?'

I don't know how he found out, but that's OK. He instilled frankness in me, so he knows when I'm lying to him. I remained silent, hoping the earth would open beneath my feet and swallow me up.

'You are no longer my son. Get out and never come back to my house.' He said these words quietly, simply. He had his back to me. I walked to the door and left, feeling like I had lost everything.

57

Upon arriving at the Centre, the children see the gifts and rush inside, despite Youssef's objection. He tells them, 'Wait at least two days!' But they fear that in two days the building will be bombed and the presents will be reduced to ashes. Josephine reassures them: everything will be moved to safety.

'If you want, we can hide the toys with us. We have a well-protected cellar,' a ten-year-old boy tells her.

'Thanks, but they're fine here,' she answers as she places the packages into bags.

'As for me, I like the drawings. I draw a lot, and my parents love what I do.'

The child takes a sheet of paper from his pocket, on which is drawn a bombed terrace, guns, and a face in the sky. 'This is my friend Ibrahim, he left last month, he is in Heaven now. He is a martyr.'

Night falls quickly over the city, the trees are frozen over. In the streets, rare passers-by buy bread at the only bakery still open. Their footsteps on the dry leaves break the silence that envelops the neighbourhood.

Bilal is in a meeting with the leader of the Islamist military group; the latter is seated in the heart of the room and grinds his long beard. 'They will not be allowed to sing or say Merry Christmas. Only then will they be allowed to protest.'

He continues by reciting this Quranic verse: '"Allah does not love those who rejoice." God here condemns all happiness foreign to Islam. This Christian holiday that you want to celebrate is not like us.' Brandishing a Quran, he says, 'And then, the music will not overthrow the regime, but this will!'

'You are right!' Bilal concedes.

'I don't want you to tell me that I'm right, I want you to believe me. We have been ruled by a criminal for fifty years. Communists and secularists tried to resist by asking for help from the international community and to what end? Al-Assad has killed and arrested tens of thousands of people. No one other than Allah will help us.'

'You are right.'

58

From: Youssef <youssefcadi@gmail.com>

Sent: 26 December 2011

To: Mohammad <mohammadamir@gmail.com>

Subject: Following up on our first meeting

My mother called me today, the intelligence services came to her house to arrest me. She begged me not to come over or call them. I know I am safe here in al-Khaldiya, but I am afraid they will take her hostage.

The situation became very complicated: a man from our neighbourhood infiltrated the Alawite zone and hid next to a general's house. When the latter got out of his car, the man stabbed him in the stomach. In retaliation, the regime executed ten prisoners in Homs and did everything to arrest activists for revenge.

Watch out for yourself, Mohammad! I've heard that the regime employs cyber specialists to monitor activists' accounts and those who contact them, even when they use VPNs. It would be best if we wrote to each other less often.

What happened between you and your father is not the end of the world. Somehow, he would have found out eventually. Our families do not accept us as we are; for that, we would need to be but simple reproductions of them. We will be persecuted because of our difference.

I know you're not happy but let me wish you a merry Christmas anyway.

59

When the officer arrives in the prison that morning, his first request is for prisoner number 117 to be brought to him.

'In my office immediately.'

'Right away,' the secretary replies, saluting. Khalil gets up when he hears his number that has replaced his first name here. The computer scientist also gets up and hugs him.

'Good luck. If you should not come back, know that I will honour our agreement.'

'Get moving and shut your ugly mouth!' the soldier rushes him along. 'Your fellows have started to assassinate the high army chiefs,' he said, addressing Khalil. 'Is this your peaceful revolution?'

Khalil opens and then closes his mouth in a futile attempt to answer. His lips are parched, there are large black circles round his eyes. His back is hunched, he wobbles, his knees keep giving way under his bruised body. The contact of the carpet under his raw feet is unbearable, he almost jumps, shaking with nervous tremors.

'Those who kill to achieve their ends are the Islamists. We have nothing to do with them.'

'We know you work together! You are all traitors!'

He shows him a photo of Youssef.

'What do you know about this asshole?'

'Nothing.'

'I have no time to waste. Either you talk or I call Dracula.'

'No! No, not him.'

'So?'

'I don't know anything about this guy! I swear to you.'

The torturer grabs him and throws him to the ground.

'This time, it's not a bottle you're going to have in your ass. Twenty soldier cocks will fuck you one after the other until tomorrow morning.'

As he crushes Khalil's shin with his boot, Khalil yells, 'Wait! Wait! Stop.'

He sobs, 'Youssef is a member of Qalb . . . He organizes demonstrations.'

His voice is just a breath. The officer straightens him up and brutally sits him down on a chair.

'Where does he live?'

'In al-Khaldiya.'

'What about the bitch named Josephine who hangs out with him all the time?' The question feels like a bullet entering his heart.

'I don't know her.'

The officer strikes him in the shin again, making him cry out. 'In that case, I'll call our friend Dracula.'

During these moments, Khalil again sees the image of Josephine the day they parted and she left for the al-Hamidiyah souk. He remembers that strange feeling that overwhelmed him for a short while.

The feeling of having already lived those moments, already seen Josephine turning her head in this charming way—yes, he had been through it before, but he had forgotten when.

The words come out; he speaks without paying attention to what he says.

'Josephine travels between Homs and Damascus, where we last saw each other. She mustn't have moved.'

The soldier takes a big sip of his coffee and thinks, looking at the sheets of paper littering the desk.

'I know you want to go out. And I promise you will go back to college. If you want money, we'll be there too. But first, you have to do what I ask you: I will give you back your cell phone. You will call Josephine and tell her that you've been released and that you're waiting for her somewhere in the city centre, and . . .'

'Out of the question!'

'Dracula . . .'

'No! It's OK. I'll do it.'

'Josephine? Hi Hi Hi! I'm free!'

'What? Since when? Where are you?'

'I'm waiting for you in front of the al-Hamidiyah souk. I'll explain everything.'

'I'm in Homs.'

The officer tells Khalil what to say.

'I'm coming then. Can you be at the bus station in two hours?'

'I'll be there. I miss you a lot.'

Once Khalil hangs up, the officer turns off the cell phone before grabbing his chin.

'Why did you say hi three times?'

'Oh, did I?'

'If it's a code between you, you're a dead man.'

60

From: Mohammad <mohammadamir@gmail.com>

Sent: 28 December 2011

To: Youssef <youssefcadi@gmail.com>

Subject: Following up on our first meeting

I can't write you any less, I'm addicted to your words. And I'm no longer afraid of being arrested for it.

You are probably surprised, but I feel immensely lonely. I think a lot about my friends who have emigrated, are imprisoned or have been involved in the revolution. All have moved away from me because I don't share their struggle.

I went to a newly opened nightclub in Bab Touma, just five kilometres from eastern Ghouta where the fighting is taking place. It's very different from the nightclubs we know: no dirty songs or prostitutes, and the decor is Western. It was full of people dancing in groups. This frenzy made it seem like they were making up for living each day with death. At the bar, a customer asked the waitress where she was from. She told him that she was displaced from around Damascus. She had fled the clashes with her family.

With her tourism diploma, she could have gone abroad, but she chose to stay: 'I'm like a fish: out of the water it can't breathe.'

I ordered a shot of vodka, I needed strong alcohol to drown out my sadness. A tall, slim, charming young man was swaying his hips near the DJ. He looked a lot like you. Further down on the dance floor, two girls were waving half-drunk. I walked over, but one of them gave me a funny look before turning away contemptuously. They continued to touch each other's faces, shoulders and breasts. Then a man bumped into me from behind and didn't even apologize. I went to order another drink, smiling at the bartender who didn't notice me. I then said goodnight to a red-haired woman who was next to me. She gave me a vague nod. I needed to talk to someone. So, I invited her over for a drink, but she immediately told me that she was engaged. The sound of the music was almost unbearable. Lights of all colours burst in beams and people continued to dance and drink without restraint. I understood from their way of being and their outfits that they were either traffickers or children of high-ranking officers.

I hated my life.

I went to the bathroom, on the wall there was an advert for sports shoes: a jogger in the middle of the desert with a bright sun above him. I touched the image with my fingertips, I imagined myself in the Arabian Peninsula, digging my hands into the sand to bury this cursed land from which only oil, wars, and hatred sprang.

At two in the morning, I came home with the need to write to you. I was desperate, devastated. In the street there was only an old man sweeping up what passers-by had thrown away.

61

The sun pierces through the curtain. Mohammad thinks back to what he said to Youssef when he was there: 'I dream of living with a cute and calm girl, who would accept me for who I am. She could be employed in an association where she would work all day. We would only see each other in the evening and go out for a walk. We would talk about everything. Then we would come home and I would make a salad while we have a drink. With her, I wouldn't need anything else. We would hardly argue . . .'

Youssef then cut him off: 'You watch too many movies these days.'

He laughs as he remembers that last comment. Then what happened between him and his father comes back to him. Just for a moment he feels free, no longer afraid of the future and no longer sad.

Headache and dizziness take over him, he cannot find sleep. He has run out of medicine, but he is reluctant to take to the streets at this hour when people are going to work.

The pharmacy is only at the end of the street. He goes out yawning, passes two young men. One of them says, 'What's up, faggot?' Without thinking, Mohammad slaps him. The two guys knock him to the ground and kick him before running away once his face is covered in blood.

Mohammad tries to stand up but fails. He crawls to the pavement where he sits for a while, his head in his hands.

A simple-minded guy whom everyone in the neighbourhood knows approaches him. As is his habit, he is holding a bottle with a sponge in it.

'Don't worry! Many have hit me too. Where are you from?'

'Damascus.'

'Me too! I am of Chinese origin and my mother is from Korea. We are all children of this sick planet.'

With a handkerchief, Mohammad wipes the blood that has run down his neck.

'But you are Syrian.'

'I'm not sure! You know, the Mongols invaded us centuries ago and they fucked our mothers. We are their offspring, which means we are bastards. Believe me, if it weren't the case, you wouldn't be seeing all this evil around you.'

He pats Mohammad's arm.

'I've been looking for a knife for a while, do you have one?'

'To do what?'

'To get the sponge out.'

'But who put it in the bottle?'

'I did. I wanted to keep it safe. I didn't know I was imprisoning this sponge. I have to release it so that peace prevails.'

Then he starts running and shouting: 'Get ready! A black hole will swallow you up!'

62

Youssef enters the room, anxious. 'You mustn't go to the station, there are some weird things going on there. I asked around and it seems no one has seen Khalil. It's a trap. You are being watched. Give me your SIM card, I'll destroy it.'

Josephine hands him the card already cut into small pieces: 'It's already done. I guessed it from his voice. We had set up a code: if one of us repeats a word on the phone, it means we have to do the opposite.' She stops and watches Youssef. The Santa Claus costume he is wearing makes him look silly, it's way too short for him, and the white beard doesn't completely cover his own. 'You look like a caricature!' she tells him, putting on her own red suit. They arrive at the plaza, where the protest is to take place, in a pickup truck decorated with multicoloured lights and filled with bags of gifts. The children are already waiting for them impatiently with their parents.

The power has been cut and four bearded armed men surround the crowd. Furious, Youssef asks them what they are doing there. One of the men explains that they are protecting the demonstratotrs on the orders of their leader.

'But we didn't ask you for anything,' Youssef replies before turning on his heels. A placard hanging on his chest reads: 'I am prisoner Khalil, accused of loving freedom.' He rings a bell and Josephine begins to sing 'Leylet Eid': 'It's Christmas Eve, Christmas Eve / The ornaments, the people, the sound of bells ringing in the distance . . .' She distributes the gifts to the children who surround her, joining in the song along with their mothers. One of them gives her a green shawl, saying, 'That's all we can offer you. I hope you like it.' Josephine wraps the shawl around her shoulders, grabs one end of it and waves it while dancing.

The bearded leader arrives and asks her to disperse the crowd immediately.

'We're not done distributing the gifts yet.'

But he insists: 'You will give out the last gifts later.'

Bilal, standing with the children's fathers, witnesses this scene between Mrs Claus and the armed man.

The children have started fighting over the packages, their parents cannot calm them down. Chaos reigns. 'Calm down!' Josephine shouts, repeating the most famous slogans of the revolution: 'Liberty, justice, democracy, pacifism!' But no one pays her any attention. Youssef wraps his arms around her and leads her to the car. His little sign 'I am prisoner Khalil' has fallen into the fray.

The Islamist leader fires in the air to restore order. 'Go home immediately!' A bullet smashes a glass door to a nearby balcony.

He asks his underlings for a can of petrol and empties every last drop onto the remaining toys before setting fire to them. Then he turns to Bilal: 'We told you songs were forbidden.'

'Believe me, I spoke to them but Josephine . . .'

'Who is this bitch who stands up to us and opposes our orders? Take me to their Centre.'

The square is lit only by the flames of the gifts going up in smoke. In this light, the men look like ghosts in the night.

63

Everywhere the noise of violence, insults, and people crying. That night, a torture concert is held in the prison. Khalil is alone again, the cold is unbearable. In the collective cell, the prisoners' breath eased it, but tonight his hands are blue, the blood in his veins has stopped flowing.

He tries to dream for a minute, even a second, that he's with Josephine. He covers his ears to make the memory of this first hour of 2012 last a bit longer. He thinks of a story he heard long ago: Saul, the evil one, was walking down the road to Damascus when a bolt of lightning flashed in the sky. Jesus spoke to Saul and ordered him to enter the city and go up to Right Street where he was to meet Hananiya, who had previously been informed by Christ of the meeting. Khalil is there, in Bab Sharqi. He runs towards his love. Josephine is in the middle of the storm. She wears a lined jacket. For him, the beauty of the universe is hidden under her clothes. Her hair is soaked. Kohl runs down her cheeks, leaving black streaks. Khalil wonders if Josephine is crying or if it's the rain. He calls out, the sky is lit by fireworks. Jasmine flowers flutter delicately, mixed with bird feather. Khalil cannot move forward, excruciating pain flows through his chest, a guard had punched him and broken a bone.

Dracula leads him into the office. The officer is comfortably seated with his feet on the table next to some grilled meat and an empty glass. In the centre of the room, two women are trembling.

'I've been told you haven't celebrated the New Year yet. Here is the opportunity for us to celebrate it together.'

He motions with his head to the young women while scrutinizing Khalil. He tries to undress them, but they bite his hand. The man pulls out a knife and rips their clothes. Khalil turns his head away. The officer laughs heartily. 'Are you embarrassed? Come on, I'm sure you miss sex. You are young, you must satisfy your impulses. Dracula, help him undress!'

Khalil doesn't move as the soldier carries out the order, forcing him to keep his eyes wide open.

The chief strokes the buttocks of his prisoners with his whip: 'See, it's nice. These two charming young women are sisters, their father deserted the army to fight on the side of the bastards.'

He grabs the smaller one by the neck and pushes her onto the table. 'Save me! I am a mother of three children!'

'I'll make you a fourth one, then!' He answers, holding her by the waist as she tries to wriggle out of his grip. He takes out his penis and begins to penetrate her.

'Take that, bitch! I'll fill you with my sperm and I'll fuck your revolution, your freedom!' Her attempts to resist him excite him even more.

Her sister yells: 'Leave her, you piece of shit! Criminal!'

'Come and take her place!'

He wedges the second sister against the wall. In the commotion, she headbutts him on the nose. He slaps her so hard that she falls to the carpet.

'Come on, you pig. I am your mother. Come fuck your mother!' She opens her thighs and, with a provocative gaze, adds, 'See how delicious her pussy is?'

The officer walks away from her, sits down and lights a cigarette. 'You ruined the mood.' He cocks his pistol, points the barrel at her. 'If I kill you, you'll be more peaceful. But first, I want you to long for death.'

He orders Dracula to take them all back to their cells.

Once alone, Khalil recalls the story of the children of Daraa who wrote on a wall: 'The people want to overthrow the regime.' It was at the start of the revolution; the intelligence services arrested them and broke their fingers. Their fathers had gone to ask General Atef Najib for their release, but he replied, 'Forget them and make other children. If you can't, send us your wives.'

64

Josephine takes care of Youssef, who suffered an arm injury during the altercation at the protest. He tells her again, 'We may not have made it all the way to the end, but we have done something important.' She shoots back at him bitterly, 'Happy New Year, dear optimist! I am very sad for these people. Did you see how they were? They fight for almost nothing.'

Footsteps reach them from outside. Youssef opens the door and finds himself facing the militia leader, his hand on his pistol and a keffiyeh wrapped around his head and forehead. His long beard reaches down to the collar of his black jacket. Bilal stands behind the man. Youssef tries in vain to remain calm; his dark eyes reveal his anger. Their eyes meet in the twilight. The militia leader pushes Youssef aside and walks into the apartment. Without a word, he walks through the Centre to the makeshift dispensary, then he observes the room where Josephine and Youssef sleep on two mattresses pushed together. 'May Allah forgive us!' he says as he walks towards the main room.

'I remind you that we are Muslims, and that religion comes first for us. You broke this basic rule.'

His shadow on the ground quivers with the flickering intensity of the candle flame. Youssef slowly takes off the Santa Claus jacket he was still wearing. 'We sang, it's not a crime.'

'It was forbidden, the order we gave was clear.'

'Just because we were all born in this country doesn't mean we have to be alike. Let us resist our way and you do what is right for you. We all have the same enemy: Bashar al-Assad, that's the most important thing today.'

'I refuse to hear this empty speech recited by a layperson.'

'As you wish, but I have the right to say it.'

'You did worse than singing tonight, your friend didn't put on a veil during the demonstration. Didn't you know it's haram?'

'She was wearing a Christmas hat,' Youssef replies with a smile.

'Are you kidding me?'

'No. Just tell yourself that this girl has brought all the medicine we needed, she has also brought in cameras. What does it matter if she covers her hair or not?'

'It's up to us to decide if it matters! We protect the neighbourhood and, for that reason alone, you must respect our rules. And then how can you two sleep in the same room when you're not married!'

'There is nothing between us.'

'That doesn't change anything, you must get married. I am an imam, I can arrange this. Here are the witnesses,' he said, pointing to his helpers. Youssef raises his eyebrows; wrinkles appear on his forehead.

'Are you serious?'

'I'm not here to joke. We can do this tonight.'

'What if we refuse?'

'You leave.'

Seated between the two men, Bilal speaks for the first time since their arrival: 'Our leader, you have a big heart! Give him two days to think it over.'

'If you're the one asking, then I'll give them the next two days.'

65

Josephine, sitting quietly in the next room, had heard it all.
She takes Youssef's hand and says mockingly, 'My husband
according to Sharia law, I will be obedient.'

'They are serious. We have forty-eight hours to make
up our minds.'

'I'm going back to Damascus tomorrow.'

'You are wanted! You are in great danger.'

'I'd rather be arrested than live with these idiots under
their laws.'

She combs her hair back.

'Since my last stay in Homs, where I saw that these bar-
barians were everywhere, I sensed a great massacre. The
current regime allows these armed and dangerous people
to do whatever they want. It gives the international community the illusion that the regime is a victim of terrorism,
so it can bomb without caring or letting anyone escape.
We, on the other hand, are nothing at all. All we wanted
was to live a human life. But we demanded freedom from
a country that was not ready.'

'This is our land.'

'Yes, but it has only offered us oppression. This country has never known stability. For centuries, we have been nothing but a war zone torn apart by dictators.'

'What is your point?'

'You must leave Syria very quickly. I'll stay and wait for Khalil.'

'You can't be useful to him in any way. And where do you want to wait? In Aleppo? Intelligence services are everywhere there. Idlib? The Muslim Brotherhood controls everything. Daraa? The city is under siege. Either we leave together, or I stay with you.'

'Only one thing scares me: that we'll forget the revolution and spend our lives lost between countries and continents.'

The candle is going out. Outside, the wind is blowing hard. Youssef turns his head towards the door. 'We were born exiles. At least, abroad, we will be officially migrants— we will no longer suffer this double exile. Let's go to Beirut. There are secret paths, we can be there in two hours.'

He pulls out his cell phone to contact the smugglers but pauses: 'Who's going to film the victims here if we leave?'

'YouTube is full of corpses, and what has that changed?'

'You know, every time I see someone who's been wounded or a bombed-out house, I think of the Spanish Civil War. Do you know of *Guernica*?'

'That sounds familiar.'

'Pablo Picasso painted a picture of a city erased from the map by the Nazis. The painting has become immensely famous. People from all countries come to contemplate it. Imagine if Picasso lived during our civil war today, how many *Guernica*s would he have to make then?'

'And even if he did, do you think that would get anyone to think of us? We have thousands of photos that document very precisely all the crimes committed by the regime. They are seen by thousands of people on the Internet. Despite all this, hardly anyone pays attention to this massacre. Our blood has no value.'

66

He spends the afternoon raving in his sleep and repeating names, especially that of his mother Suad, and Josephine's. When Khalil wakes up, he feels like he has had a thousand nightmares forgotten upon awakening.

Someone knocks on the wall of the next cell. At first, he thinks it's a hallucination, but five minutes later the noise starts again. Khalil responds with a single knock on his side of the wall. Two taps answer him. He knows there is only one inmate in this cell. He'd only glimpsed the person once, unable to determine if it was a man or a woman. He curls up a little more in the dark.

He taps the wall rhythmically; the answer comes back to him in the same way. This dialogue continues until morning. The hallway is empty and silence reigns in the prison.

When the guard arrives, Khalil gives two sharp taps to wish his neighbour good night. He doesn't know if his neighbour understood.

For days, the torture has stopped, and they bring Khalil rice instead of potatoes. Oftentimes he tells himself that he really wants to eat a tomato dish. He misses the scent of this fruit more than its taste. Just thinking about it, he hears the songs of his village. A stream of saliva rushes into his mouth, he takes a very deep breath, an aura of summer morning clouds his soul. At this point, he would be ready to give his life for a tomato.

67

From: Youssef <youssefcadi@gmail.com>

Sent: 01 January 2012

To: Mohammad <mohammadamir@gmail.com>

Subject: Following up on our first meeting

I can't explain everything to you. I'm leaving for Beirut in a little while. Can you join me there?

Lebanon will not be my final destination. I don't want to live in a country where the Syrians have no rights. We will only stay there for a few days, maybe a month, before applying for asylum in France.

We, 23 million Syrians, live as migrants inside our own country, and double that outside it. We are scattered all over the earth: from Latin America to China. Historically, we have always managed to form a homeland only outside our own soil.

I will arrive before sunset. On the road I'll think of your lips, your voice, your neck and your breath when you make love to me. They will give me the energy to cross the border.

I'm waiting for the driver, which gives me a little time to inscribe all the details of this neighbourhood in my memory. Here, in the midst of danger, I have lived a thousand lives.

68

From: Mohammad <mohammadamir@gmail.com>

Sent: 02 January 2012

To: Youssef <youssefcadi@gmail.com>

Subject: Following up on our first meeting

I have been waiting for you for months in Damascus and you invite me to Lebanon!

Our country separates us, but exile will reunite us. What a sur-real life!

I had a little accident, and for a few days I didn't leave my house. I gathered my things. But since I have a lot of books, I can't take them with me. I wrapped them in a sheet and went down to the garden behind the building where I buried them. I didn't do this to turn them into a book tree, but to protect them from future bombings. Maybe someone will find them someday, someone who will know that words are mightier than weapons.

I'll leave the key at home. I won't say goodbye to anyone. Anyway, everyone I know has disappeared. I will travel by plane.

It will be less painful than seeing the places where I grew up. I don't want to remember anything.

I believe that we will all end up, down to the last Syrian, meeting elsewhere, outside the country. For those who remain, the Syria we know will eventually abandon them too.

And yes, this tragedy is not new. For a long time, we have been driven out by Islamic conquests, battles between the Caliphs, Mongols, Ottomans, by coups—and here's history repeating itself, but with the fascists. I am sure that a thousand years ago people lived like us, rejecting this violence, and ended up either being killed or fleeing.

This war is like the Roman games in which men fought to the death. The difference now is that the spectator is the rest of the world. Eventually, killers and those killed will disappear, only their forgotten graves will be left. There will be no one here to remember their time.

In the midst of this complete collapse, all that matters is our history.

69

They don't have a lot to pack. Youssef hides in a shoe a memory card containing everything he has filmed since the beginning of the revolution. Josephine wants to take everything with her: the curtains, the blankets, even the words spoken in this room. Suddenly, while packing, she says, 'It's true that we didn't get married under their Sharia law. But I have the feeling that we got married our own way. We refused their marriage to choose ours. It's not a metaphor—I see it, I feel it. It is a strong, sacred marriage, the time we have spent between these walls has created an eternal bond between us.'

'I can feel it too. It's a marriage between rebels. Perhaps a new generation of rebels will come and continue our resistance.'

'Or we'll be the ones to come back and complete what we started.'

The departure is final, but nobody dares to admit it.

On leaving the Centre, they meet an old man and his wife. The latter puts her hand on Josephine's arm: 'I know they won't leave you in peace, but we'll protect you. We feel safe thanks to you.'

'It's too late, there's no more room for us here. We don't want to cause you problems.'

The old man looks at them. 'The ship is sinking, and you are birds. Go build your nest in the distance.'

Bilal stands next to the car, trying to apologize for what happened. Youssef angrily closes the boot: 'Either you go with us now, or you continue here with these brutes.'

'Lower your voice!'

'Is this the revolution you dream of?'

The sound of bullets coming from afar cuts off their conversation for a moment before dissipating quickly.

'I can't back down any longer. I have pledged my allegiance to the imam, they will kill me wherever I go.'

'If you apply for asylum, you will be protected.'

'I am a devoted believer, I cannot deny my faith, even if I don't agree with everything they do.'

The vehicle starts, Josephine gazes one last time at the balconies, the doors and the half-destroyed walls. Each contains hundreds of stories, secrets, hopes—those of a country in suffering. Youssef points to the swing, the shell that the children were swaying is still there. Next to it, the children are playing marbles with piles of empty cartridge cases. Josephine waves her green shawl as a farewell but, too engrossed in their game, they don't notice her.

70

In a corner of the room, a small black stone, basalt, seems foreign in the midst of its grey companions. An ant appears on its surface and goes, before climbing the wall, descending, then disappearing.

Khalil thinks about the day of his release. He wishes to return to the collective cell, where the discussions soothe him. But no, on the contrary, it wouldn't let him freely surrender to his fantasies.

He is with Josephine, on the mountain of Qasioun, both sitting and facing Damascus. The city seems to them immense and calm. It stretches as far as the eye can see, speckled with the shimmer of small lights. Khalil tries to locate his house. A group dressed in white walks past them, gazing up at the sky without paying attention to anyone. He scans their faces: it's Rachid, Bilal, Youssef, Adel and others whom he met during this lifetime.

A woman is crying. The sound of chains and the guards' footsteps brings him out of his reverie. Doors open and close, the ant has returned. Is it the same or another? He offers her a grain of rice: the insect takes it and goes away, free. He grabs the small black stone and writes at the bottom of the wall: 'O you who are going to pass by here, what's hardest is the prison within you.'

The song of a nightingale reaches him through the small window. The bird hops between the bars.

He and Josephine come down from the mountain, the town is empty as if it were theirs. The books are still on the pavements of al-Halbouni; the vendors sleep nearby. A tree is marked with a trace of black smoke: A bomb? Or a fire somebody lit to warm themselves?

They arrive at the place where they had kissed. Dawn is breaking behind the mountain, the tiny crescent moon is still visible, and a star is shining beyond the Old Town.

In front of a large fountain, lilies stretch their stems as if to tell passers-by their story. One of the blossoms has been cut and thrown to the ground. Khalil picks it up and puts it in Josephine's hair. She turns away like the last time, but from now on, he is sure that she will not go away any more. He is with her forever on this endless path.

Intermondes Centre
La Rochelle
19 August 2018